AN LA TO LA COZY MYSTERY BOOK 1

Bad Blood
in the Bayou

'FRAMED'

JULIE BELMONT

Book Cover by Julie Belmont

Illustrations by Julie Belmont

Edited by John De Lorez

First Edition 2023

Night Raven Publishing

4770 Eureka Ave. #301

Yorba Linda, California 92885—USA

ISBN: 978-0-9755984-1-2

I dedicate this book to those who don't settle for answers like
"Just because."
They have intelligent and curious minds who love to be part of the
mystery solving.
And most of all, want to laugh along the way.
I hope you enjoy reading this book as much as
I enjoyed writing it.

Contents

1. Chapter 1   1
   New Beginnings

2. Chapter 2   5
   Resentful Bride

3. Chapter 3   11
   Something is Missing

4. Chapter 4   15
   To Help or Hinder

5. Chapter 5   20
   Good Cop, Bad Cop

6. Chapter 6   23
   Need to Talk

7. Chapter 7   27
   Elephant in the Room

8. Chapter 8   38
   Hello, detective

9. Chapter 9   44
    Nothing like a Beignet

10. Chapter 10   49
    Time of Discovery

11. Chapter 11   54
    No Upper Hand

12. Chapter 12   58
    Meeting of the Minds and Hearts

13. Chapter 13   62
    Mournful over Murder

14. Chapter 14   66
    The List

15. Chapter 15   72
    Lies and Deceit

16. Chapter 16   76
    The Apothecary

17. Chapter 17   81
    Night Mission

18. Chapter 18   87
    Enlightenment with Luminol

19. Chapter 19   91
    Blood Findings

20. Chapter 20   95
    Tears Emerge

21. Chapter 21   100
    Jac's Place

22. Chapter 22   106
    Into the Bayou

23. Chapter 23   110
    From Shots to Chats

24. Chapter 24   116
    Enough Talk, Gotta Go!

25. Chapter 25   120
    No Bullet Holes?

26. Chapter 26   125
    Civil Approach

27. Chapter 27   133
    Behind the Glass

28. Chapter 28   139
    Jail Bird

29. Chapter 29   142
    What's your Emergency?

30. Chapter 30   148
    What a Ride

31. Chapter 31   154
    Hospital Safety

32. Chapter 32   162
    Jambalaya Comfort

33. Chapter 33   166
    Point of Entry

34. Chapter 34   173
    Whisper Mode

35. Chapter 35   178
       Covert Duo

36. Chapter 36   184
       The Ticking Clock

37. Chapter 37   190
       One more question

38. Chapter 38   196
       Run!

Characters   201
   In order of appearance

JESSICA MARTIN   203

ROBERT HUNT   204

ANTOINE DUBOIS   205

CONSTANTINE CARRON   206

DET. LOUIS LACROIX   207

CECILIA ROGERS   208

THOMAS DUPRIS   209

TC aka Tiny Cat   210

TK Tiny K9   211

Also by this Author   212

Bad Blood in the Bayou 'Wide-Angle' Book 2   213
The Venue

Acknowledgements   217

In Closing   218

Chapter 1

New Beginnings

The early morning light is cresting over the Tupelo Gum Trees and the Bald Cypress known as the Sentinels of the Swamp. I'm in awe at the beauty. I am so glad I have returned to Louisiana, where I yearned to be for so long. My career as a forensic photographer has taken me away to major cities all over. Being good at something can be both a blessing and a curse. I worked with one of the most elite crime labs in the country, based in Los Angeles. The nameplate engraved with Jessica Martin—Forensics Department, hung on the door, and the world's weight hung on my shoulders.

Strolling along the water's edge in my beloved Bayou, I most appreciate my walking stick. In this swampy, uneven terrain, it isn't a fashion statement but a must. It is necessary to stay upright, which I do, especially if I want to outrun the alligators and other local critters.

My late uncle Stephan carved my handy and elaborate cane. He was an artist who put his soul into his art. He has been long gone. My biggest regret is not being there for him on his last days due to my job. Surrounded by the greenery in the humid marsh, I can feel his essence around me as if he is walking by my side. By having the walking stick he lovingly made, I will always have a piece of him with me.

Sitting on a rock, I sip water from my canteen. My faithful canteen was given to me by a dear friend who, unfortunately, lost her life in the line of duty. I just realized that things I hold dear are from people who are dead. This is interesting and a little weird- something to ponder on for another day or not.

Let's concentrate on what I came here to do. My outing is to take pictures to sell to Antoine DuBois—the owner of NOLA Tourist Tours. He uses my photos for advertising in his brochures and website. Antoine is the hub for all the tours in the area. He has connections with everyone: the steamboat harbor cruise, the airboats, the haunted mansions, you name it, he has his hands and wallet in it. I like the variety of assignments; it keeps it exciting. So glad I'm back in my hometown.

Speaking of back, back to work, pictures don't take themselves. This time of the morning, the shadows are still soft and at the right angle. Closer to noon, forget it; the light is harsh and unforgiving. Well, perhaps not as unforgiving as I am of my work. I've been called a perfectionist on more than one occasion. That can be good, but when you work with a team and demand the same caliber of work from everyone, it can ruffle more than a few feathers.

One thing about walking around the bush and taking pictures is that it gives one time to reflect on things. Does my desire for perfection distance me from others? Do I hold people to such high standards they feel discarded and unwanted? I have friends, like my bestie Renee

Dolton. She's always been there for me. We met in third grade, and she has put up with me all these years. Even when I was traveling or working on a case—she was the one to call at all hours. She would listen while I described the gruesome scenes I was exposed to. Visions you see whether your eyes are opened or closed. It helps that Renee is a mortician at her family's funeral home. To her, death is part of her life.

Where did the time go? I have enough pictures, for now, I must run well, tread carefully in the deep-rooted and marshy ground. I'll return tomorrow at daybreak to capture some exceptionally soft images, only available as the sun rises and the ground fog remains. It's a glorious time of the day when the nocturnal creatures go to slumber and the Bayou fully awakens.

I am running when I hit the gravel area where I parked my trusty Jeep Cherokee Trailhawk. I don't want to be late for my appointment with the Bride of all Brides, Ms. Maryellen Smith. She could be challenging, to say the least. I wouldn't want to start the meeting on the wrong foot by being late. She doesn't appear to be the forgiving kind.

I rush home while observing all the speed laws, right?

I quickly select what I'm going to wear to the meeting. My favorite red cotton blouse, clean jeans, and grey ankle boots—now, where are my socks? I just had them here. I look up and see TK, my six-pound terrier (monkey dog.) She's dragging my socks into the kitchen. She stops for a moment to ensure I'm following her and then runs to her food and water bowl. She looks up at me with contempt; yes, dogs have expressions, especially this one. As I approach, she drops it in the water bowl. "Ok, you got me. The water bowl is empty—don't look at me like I'm a bad doggy mama. You have four other water bowls." I plead my case. She's unhappy until I fill her favorite one and refresh her food bowl. Her tail is wagging, and all is well. I take back my sock. TC, the cat, was napping and utterly unaware of any goings-on.

Just hop in and out of the shower, dress, and put on make-up in record time. Going out the door, I grab my tablet/portfolio to show Maryellen my photo gallery. It sure beats the old portfolios with the large prints in the plastic sleeves, especially in this humid Louisiana heat. The pictures would often get ruined when the sleeves sweat and get stuck to the photos. There is no recovery from that. Nobody wants to see or smell moldy pictures.

Chapter 2

Resentful Bride

Here I am at the cozy Mon Cherie Coffee Shop. I love this place at the edge of the French Quarter. The aroma of freshly baked pastries is so delightful. I'm sitting with my back up against the wall with a clear sight of both entrances. (I've been working with cops for too long.) I wait for the bride-to-be and her maid of honor, Annie Jones. Just as the clock strikes one o'clock, they burst into the place. This should be fun; they seem agitated, and I haven't even told them my fee.

I greet them with my best welcoming smile and hope to de-escalate their feisty mood.

"Maryellen, you're going to make a beautiful bride," I say.

"I'm sure you say that to all the brides," Maryellen replies with a smirk.

"Yes, but sometimes, I mean it."

"Well, enough of the pleasantries, I haven't got all day."

"Of course, Maryellen, we'll get to it right away. I'd like to show you my portfolio with different styles and location shoots for the photos before the wedding, the wedding itself, the reception, and any other specific photos you may want to have to celebrate your special day."

She is swiping her fingers through the screen so fast that it is no longer a gallery of pictures but an entire movie viewed at high speed. She's giving me no time to describe the shots or get her opinion.

Great...Here comes the waiter with the soft, warm, and buttery croissants. What a contrast to the thick tension you can cut with a knife. I'm looking at Annie with pleading eyes. Perhaps she can intercede and calm her friend, who seems on the verge of a meltdown.

Annie reaches over and takes the tablet from Maryellen's trembling hands.

"Maryellen, relax, take a breath. This is all supposed to be fun and wonderful," Annie says.

"I can't relax, not after what that idiot, Antoine, put me through the other day," Maryellen says, holding back tears.

Wow! I'm not ready for this. But I am curious about what poor Antoine did to cause such pain and anguish.

Maryellen takes a deep breath and starts explaining what happened with Antoine DuBois.

"Two days ago, I had an appointment with that caricature of a man. I had arranged and contracted the Rose Queen steam riverboat for my reception."

"That's a gorgeous boat, you have fantastic taste." I'm wishing praise would go a long way.

"I know." She speaks. "May I continue?"

"Of course, my lips are sealed." While zipping my lips and looking at Annie—who is rolling her eyes at her friend.

"Like I was saying--this time, I wanted to see the actual boat to pass the information to my designer and wedding coordinator. I have a photographic mind, so I would relay a perfectly accurate description of the place, and they could start the sketches for the décor." She explained and looked at me.

I won't comment; I just nod my approval and wait for her to continue.

"You can imagine my shock when the idiot makes me run up the stairs after him to the top level, without the slightest hesitation at the first two levels of the ship—and dares to ask--How do I like the view from the top deck? I looked around and said, it's nice, but I'm not here to look at the view. I'm here to look at the entire venue—the whole boat, all three levels. I have over three hundred guests!"

Maryellen is not releasing her pent-up frustration. Instead, she is getting all worked up.

"He messed up." Annie says, "He rented the levels or decks; I believe they're called to different parties."

I'm speechless. I know and have worked with Antoine for a while now, and he doesn't seem like a dimwit to me. Maybe a little greedy—after hearing this, obviously, very greedy.

"So, what happened?" I asked, fearing the man ended up overboard.

"Oh, it got bad, really bad. But Maryellen couldn't help herself. She just couldn't." Annie says.

Maryellen is agitated and bursting at the seams. She must tell it herself.

"I told that jerk--I could kill him; he ruined my wedding day. I can't have a bunch of strangers intruding on my party. I cannot share the boat; the boat is for me and my guests."

She takes a sip of her iced tea; I'm sure wishing it was something more potent.

"The wedding is around the corner. There is no time to book anything else," Maryellen says.

"I'm so sorry to hear that." It's all I can say.

"Oh, no, that's not the end of it. Antoine dared to say there was one more thing, a slight detail he felt he needed to disclose."

I'm enthralled in all this, but the thought of discussing my fees keeps surfacing. I don't think this is the best time to bring it up. Maybe another meeting? Or I suggest they put cameras on all the tables and take selfies. I'm almost ready to decline this job, but I can't do that. I realize this poor, emotional wreck of a girl doesn't need another disappointment. I snap out of my reverie just in time to say.

"What else could that scoundrel have to say?"

"He dared tell me that other parties would be on the boat, and a last-minute event would share the upper deck with my reception- a bachelor party, of all things."

Annie says. "Maryellen lost it and told Antoine he was a dead man. I've never seen her so angry,"

"I can't imagine how stressful that was. I feel it's best to reschedule a short meeting in a couple of days. I assure you there will be no issues. I'll bring all the equipment necessary to do a stellar job. We'll discuss my fees at that time. I'll call you Wednesday and confirm a time, okay?"

That went well. I knew any further discussion would be a waste at this time.

Annie smiles apologetically and says she'll call me. She escorts Maryellen out of the place before she makes a further scene. I'm left at the table to pay the bill. The good thing is, I get to take home a doggy bag. TK and TC love croissants.

I'm shaken, if not stirred, by the meeting and all the tension. I need to call Renee and see if she'll meet me for a beverage of the adult kind.

I'm calling as I walk to the jeep. She answers on the first ring. I don't even say hello. I dive right in. "Renee, where are you, girl? Do you have time for an afternoon refreshment?"

"Where and when?" she says without hesitation.

"Lafitte's in 15 minutes?" The line clicks off, and she'll be there.

Lafitte's Blacksmith Shop Bar is its actual name. It's been in the same place on Bourbon Street in the French Quarter since around 1720. It's dark, dingy, and just what I need to cheer me up.

Like clockwork, Renee pulls up at the same time I do.

"Am I glad to see you!"

"Okay, what happened with the bride? Is everything okay?" Renee asks.

"Let's get a cold one, and then I'll tell you the whole thing, including the death threats," I say teasingly.

I'm explaining the whole thing about the crazy event to Renee. She's listening patiently. She's a great friend. She loves to listen, take it all in, break it up, and add humor. I don't know how she does it, but I'm feeling much better when I'm finished telling her the predicament.

I'm a light drinker, so we're ordering food and chatting about all kinds of things. We need to catch up. We agree that Antoine better not show up at the reception unless he wants to high dive off the top deck.

"I can imagine Maryellen tossing the man overboard after a few drinks," Rene says jokingly.

We laugh at the cartoonish image and continue peeling and eating the crawfish.

Time flies when you're having fun and a good conversation. The tension of the day has disappeared. It is time to say goodbye.

As I drive home, I plan where to get my idyllic photos. As soon as I get home and feed my little munchkins, I'll be ready to relax for the evening. Read a bit and watch one of my favorite Mystery Movies. I'll be getting to bed early. I'm so exhausted from all the meeting's tension that I'll be dead asleep as soon as my head hits the pillow. My slumber will be deep and welcoming.

Chapter 3

Something is Missing

There is nothing like waking up to the radio playing Bourbon Street Parade. Talk about jumping out of bed. This band makes you dance out of bed. And if the music doesn't wake you up, there is always the cat squeaky toy I'm stepping on. That got my heart racing. Just to keep the momentum going, let's brew some coffee. Of course, you must make the rounds, fill up the doggy and kitty bowls, and ensure they have plenty of water.

Yes, water, what an excellent and much-needed thing in this hot and humid place. Got the canteen, check! --I got my backpack with camera equipment, check! Hat, check! Walking stick--Where the heck is my walking stick? Umm! I always keep it in the same place, in the kitchen, behind the back door, within easy reach as I go out to the car. Was I in such a rush that I didn't put it where it belonged? This is ridiculous. I don't see it anywhere. It's almost daybreak. I can't lose the window of opportunity for the perfect light. Especially since I promised Antoine I would have all the pictures by later this evening. I'll take my other walking stick I keep behind the bedroom door. That will do for now, but I'm taking this place apart when I get home until I find it.

"TK, you didn't hide it somewhere, did you girl?" I yell back as I run to my ride.

***

Walking through the wilderness can be challenging, but well worth it to capture that one-of-a-kind shot. As a photographer, I observe everything through the lens. I allow my senses to guide me along the way. The archways of the trees with the hanging Spanish moss are gorgeous.

The breeze stirs, and the hairs on my neck stand up simultaneously. With the draft coming my way, a strong smell of decay reaches me. An odor I can never forget. I'm breathing through my mouth as I move forward. What kind of thing emits such a stench? I'm sure I know and hope I'm wrong. Most people would turn back, but my legs seem to have a mind of their own. My legs don't have noses. I'm pushing forward against my better judgment. My rational mind is saying whatever it was will sooner or later be consumed by the Bayou and its creatures. I've had enough of death and unforgettable horrid scenes. I don't know if my civic duty leads the way or curiosity. My morbid curiosity is winning.

There is a patch of flattened tall grass up ahead. The smell is coming from that direction. I'm committed to finding out what it is. I secure my camera and get my stick ready. There might be some critters feasting on the carcass. I'm hoping my trusty hiking post will keep them at bay or, better yet, will scare them away. The smell is getting worse. I'm taking out my bandana from the backpack and tying it around my nose and mouth. I pass the tall grass still standing to my right. I can't make out what it is lying there. It is covered with mud and leafy debris.

I've come this far; I must get closer. Ouch! What am I stepping on? A piece of wood or root-- or something? I lost my balance for an instant. Looking down and figuring out what that muddy thing is. My heart stops for a second or maybe longer. I can't believe my eyes. It's MY walking stick. How did it get here? Did I leave it behind yesterday, and an animal dragged it here? I swear I had it with me when I went home. I remember it falling because I was so hurried to meet Maryellen. I picked it up and leaned it against the wall behind the kitchen door. So, again, how did it get here and why? Focus and see what's lying by the water's edge.

I'm approaching, and the reality is sinking in. I can see it. It is a man, a dead man. I'm aware he didn't get there on his own. There are drag marks from the side of the lagoon. Somebody brought him here. I know enough not to disturb the crime scene. Carefully, I get closer to see who it is. Holding a twig, I gently remove a large leaf covering his face. I almost fall back as Antoine's cloudy gaze looks up at me.

I guess he won't be needing the pictures anymore. What am I thinking? Okay, center and think clearly. I must call the authorities; I found a dead body. I don't know how he died, but I know I will find out. I have to, I knew him, he was my friend. No cell service, of course not. It couldn't be that easy. I'll walk back. I should get cell reception in a bit. Oh yeah! About the stick.

What do I do with the stick? I could remove it from the scene. Who am I kidding? If the stick were used to commit the murder, there would be evidence. The walking stick has elaborate carvings, including

Raven's head on the handle. That alone would be an easy match to any injury—if the cause of death was blunt force trauma.

I must photograph the area to preserve any evidence that can be disturbed by anyone trudging the scene. Can't leave that to the locals. I'm taking detailed and close-up pictures of the tracks along the water's edge, or better yet, the lack of tracks—as it is a smooth, wide indent in the mud. Whatever came ashore had a flat bottom which flattened the foliage. The drag marks start at the end of the flat imprint on the muddy ground, away from the water's edge to the body's resting place. Whoever did this wanted the body to be found. Must take pictures of the stick concerning the distance to the body. Take a few more shots for good measure. I think I have what I need without contaminating the space. It's time to get cell service, contact the troops, hope they're efficient, and know what they're doing.

I have to get a hold of myself. Jessica Martin thinking of removing evidence from the scene of a crime. I know better. Now, I know I'm in shock. In what Universe would I ever consider that? Walking away from the odor and the horrific scene is helping clear my head. My stick is at the location. Somebody took it and put it there. I've been framed.

Chapter 4

To Help or Hinder

I'm leaning up against my Jeep's front fender, giving off the semblance of calm and composure. My heart betrays me, beating frantically and threatening to jump out of my chest. I must keep it together. I know the first person at the crime scene is the one who will be asked hundreds of questions. Any answer given that is not convincing enough or doesn't fit the pattern of the interrogation can be perceived as a lie. Once that's established even prematurely, it can lead to a journey down the rabbit hole. It could be the difference between freedom and incarceration. The truth may come out eventually. I don't want to play those odds.

After what seems like an eternity, I hear the faint sound of sirens approaching. I see the light bars toying with shadows on the tree-lined street as they get louder. Here they come. I take a deep breath and remind myself I just found him, and above all, I have no reason to kill him. That is the primary key—the motive.

I did mention I found a dead body on the phone. I'll always wonder why law enforcement troops drive into the parking lot at such a high speed. As the dust settles, I can determine the different agencies showing up. There is the New Orleans Police Department and the Orleans Parish Sheriff's Department, with a couple of K9s, and of course, because of the location of the Bayou Sauvage National Wildlife Refuge, a couple of Special agents from the Fish and Wildlife Service. I hope my fishing license is current...

I wonder who's going to take point on this one. Usually, when multiple agencies are involved, everything takes longer as they grandstand each other for position. All I can do is show them the scene, listen carefully, answer their questions, and hope that logic will prevail.

I move forward, ready to greet them. I don't know how to act under these circumstances. Usually, I'm the one running around taking pictures, moving people out of the way with full authority for being at the crime scene. This time, it's different, really different. I feel like an uninvited guest at my funeral.

I hate to be right sometimes. The agencies are standing a few feet away, discussing their territory, jurisdiction, who will do what, and when.

Enough of this waiting. I'm approaching and introducing myself. The only female I see in the group is one of the Special Agents with the Fish and Wildlife Service. I guess they're hanging back in case they're needed and making sure nobody tramples any of the wildlife during the removal of the victim. I'll use my standard greeting since she's out of ear range, and I don't want to seem partial to any particular agency.

"Gentlemen, I'm Jessica Martin. I discovered the body in the marsh. Would you like to follow me now so I can show you the location?"

"I'm Deputy Labatt with the Orleans Parish Sheriff's Department. And this here is Officer Jason with the New Orleans Police Department," he says with a light smile.

So far, so good. Nobody pushed my face onto the hood of a car and cuffed me.

"Due to the jurisdiction in this area, this will be a multi-agency collaboration. Of course, you don't have to worry about that." Deputy Labatt explains.

Do I detect a condescending tone? I'm so glad he is concerned about my worries. I nod and point in the direction of the path. "Shall we?" I ask and extend my hand as if inviting a group of visitors on a tour.

***

Trudging through a swamp surrounded by uniforms and K9s barking and frothing at the mouth is not my idea of fun. Walking with only the dogs and their handlers ahead of me, I feel a heaviness I can't shake in my chest. How will I explain the presence of my walking stick at the scene? I can't play dumb when they ask what that is. It will be best to tell them. Tell them it's my walking stick. It was missing from my house this morning. I had it yesterday morning when I was taking pictures. When I discovered it at the crime scene, I was beyond surprised. I am questioning how it got there myself and would appreciate their thoughts on that. Maybe they would be kind enough to help me decipher this puzzle. After all, it could be a simple explanation...such as I'm being framed—but why? That I couldn't answer; that's where the mystery will unravel and hopefully lead somewhere helpful. A place far, far away from being locked up.

I'm jarred into the present and out of my thoughts when somebody shouts my name.

"Ms. Martin, before we enter the scene—I want to take a moment and get your exact entry point into the area. Do you recall from which direction you entered the location once you saw a body on the ground?" Said Deputy Labatt.

"Yes, I remember it very well. From the path, I saw the area where the tall grass was flattened. I rounded the corner, and that's when I saw...that's when I saw the decedent."

"What did you do next?"

"I walked up to him carefully. I wanted to check to see if maybe, just maybe, he could be alive. That's when I grabbed a stick and carefully removed the leaf covering his face."

The glazed, lifeless look on Antoine's face staring up at me came flooding in. For a moment, I felt light-headed, as if I were going to pass out. I've seen many dead bodies, but it's different when you know someone.

"Are you okay?" asked Officer Jason of the NOPD.

"Yes, I'm all right. It must be the heat, and I left my water in the car. Or maybe I just realized this is somebody I know. Somebody I'd worked with."

"You know the victim?" Deputy Labatt said with renewed interest.

"Yes, that's Antoine DuBois, owner of NOLA Tourist Tours. I supply him with all the pictures for his brochures and website."

"You didn't tell us you knew the victim." Both Deputy Labatt and Officer Jason say simultaneously.

"You didn't ask," I say.

I guess there is no good time to open one's mouth and say something that will make matters go from bad to worse. Okay, here I go...

"Gentlemen! Do you see that walking stick by the bushes? That's my stick. My uncle carved it for me. You could say it is an heirloom."

"You can call it an heirloom if you like—we call it a possible murder weapon."

Chapter 5

Good Cop, Bad Cop

I am sitting on a hard metal chair in a small grey room that smells like sweat and fear. I'm sure fear has an odor or tangible energy that compels you to sweat profusely. Sometimes, doing or saying the right thing can catapult you to the wrong place. They watch my every move, facial expression, and demeanor through the one-way mirror. Even though they're not here, they're present every second. They're observing every sign of weakness, nervousness, and anxiety. Knowing the routine doesn't make it any less scary. I know getting me a bottle of cold water from the vending machine doesn't take fifteen minutes.

I also know I release my DNA for examination when I sip the water. I know my DNA is at the scene. My walking stick was there. I have a logical explanation. Somebody took it and placed it there. But I cannot explain why. Sitting here is not going to get me any answers. I must get out of here. The sooner, the better. I'm not cuffed, I'm not under arrest, I'm only here for questioning--so, they say. Just breathe and act normally. What is normal under these circumstances? When they return, I'll answer the questions to the best of my ability and take my water with me. Maybe, by letting them know how invested I am in clearing myself, I can request their help, and they will allow me to ride their coattails on the case. After all, I know people.

"Sorry to keep you waiting.' I'm Detective LaCroix, and I've been assigned to this case. Oh! Here is your water. Is there anything else I can get you?" he says with a friendly smile and a definite Southern charm.

He must be the good cop; now, where is the bad cop?

"I wouldn't say no to a pillow for this chair." I figure throwing a little charm back may go a long way.

"I'll see what I can do about that. In the meantime, let's get some of these questions out of the way. I apologize if these questions seem redundant to the ones you already answered with the deputy and officer at the scene. But I want to get my answers to be clear on all counts."

"I understand, fire away--well, don't fire, just ask."

Do I have to keep reminding myself to take a breath? This is not a time for humor. Gosh, I never thought I would think that. His demeanor changes as he shuffles through the file in front of him. I don't care for all business, just the facts, Ma'am look in his eyes. I think he's going to play both good and bad cop. Oh Boy!

"There seem to be some discrepancies in the time of death of Mr. DuBois. We'll know more once we get the results of the autopsy. Right now, we're establishing a timeline. Where were you last night?" he says.

"I was at home."

"All night?"

"Yes. I had an early shoot, I mean photo shoot, to do early in the morning, so I was in bed by 10:30 at the latest."

"Can anybody verify that?"

"I live alone, and my cat and dog are not very talkative lately, so I doubt you'll get anything from them." I can't help myself; I get sarcastic when I'm nervous. I hope he doesn't take offense.

"Is this a joke to you, Ms. Martin? There is a dead man, someone you know, and you're making light of it."

"Sorry, Detective, I was just trying to liven, oops! Wrong choice of words. Please continue."

"So, nobody can verify your whereabouts on the night of the murder?" he says.

"Not that I can think of. You'll have to take my word for it. I can tell you this. I don't have a motive for killing Mr. DuBois. He is a friend and somebody who pays me well for the pictures I provide. There is no reason for me to do him any harm whatsoever. And while you're wasting your time with me, there is a real killer out there—getting further away and leaving a colder trail behind. You don't have anything to charge me with. If I committed the crime, I wouldn't call it in. I'm out of here."

"I'm not finished." His authoritative voice lagged a bit.

"You were finished when you didn't bring me the pillow. I have a friend's killer to find."

I'm leaving the room and taking my water bottle with me. I have a phone call to make.

Chapter 6

Need to Talk

I must call Robert first thing. I know he's the one who can help me with this dilemma. Here I am in a catch-22. I understand how analytical he is. He'll need some solid facts for a lead on this. Right now, all I have is a big fat, nothing. For some reason, somebody wants to incriminate me in Antoine's murder. Why? Who do I know who wants to get rid of me or at least send me to prison? These are the answers I need to have before I call him. Or do I call him like a damsel in distress and have him help me figure it out? I think it's time to put my ego and pride aside and make the call. After all, I don't have a timeline for when the authorities may knock at my door with a warrant.

"You have reached Special Agent Hunt at the Los Angeles Federal Bureau of Investigation office. Please leave a message and clearly state your name, phone number, and reason for your call, and I'll get back to you promptly. Thank you."

Wow! That is a warm greeting. Before leaving a message, I must defrost for a minute.

"Hi Robert, it's me, Jess. I need your help. I'm in a situation down here and need to talk to you ASAP. I didn't call you on your cell as I don't want to cause any issues at home."

I hope he's not out of town on an assignment. Knowing Robert, he'll check his messages regularly—unless he's knee-deep in a case. While I wait, I'll list potential suspects who may have a motive for framing me. I thought I got along with everybody, but I was wrong. The most frightening thing was realizing someone broke into my home in the middle of the night. My sense of safety is shattered. I always double-check and make sure everything is locked. Now, I feel that's not nearly enough. Nothing else was missing. The only thing taken is my precious walking stick. TK was no help. She was sleeping soundly and oblivious to the intruders, just like me.

***

I'm awake; I'm awake! I must have dozed off while making the naughty list of those who may want to harm me. My heart is racing as I breathe and answer the phone with a degree of normalcy. As I glance at the caller ID, I'm relieved and anxious.

"Hi Robert, glad you called me back so soon."

"Not sure if you're being sarcastic-it's been at least four hours since you left the message. I was working on a case, and this is the soonest I could get back to you. Are you okay?

"I'm okay, at least for now. I don't even know where to start."

"How about the beginning? What kind of trouble did you get yourself into this time, young lady?"

I could tell he was making light and helping me relax. He knew me too well. I rarely reach out to another human being for assistance—time to share everything so he can clearly understand the circumstances.

"A friend of mine was murdered. My walking stick, which my uncle gave me, was found at the scene. Somebody is trying to frame me to take the fall for this. I have no idea why?"

"To frame somebody in a murder is a decisive and serious offense. The motive is very personal. Whoever is implicating you feels hurt, betrayed, or has lost somebody they loved because of you. Their intention is revenge. They want you to suffer the same pain—whatever that may be. An eye for an eye type of thing."

"Okay, Mr. Profiler. Is that supposed to make me feel better?"

"No, it's about making you see who would detest you so deeply, even if it's only in their delusion, to want to come after you. You have to look at your friends and acquaintances in a different light."

He was all business. I'm glad he was in my corner.

"It's not in my nature to look at my friends like suspects."

"I know you have a good heart. Even with all you've seen and been through—you still believe in the good in people. You must realize somebody is trying to frame you for murder. That's the reality you must accept to give you the perspective needed to clear yourself.

"Okay, no problem, just jotting down on my notes—Grow a backbone and treat everybody like a perp. Got it!" I say with a forced smile.

"I'll fly out there in the morning. We want to be one step ahead—things like this can get out of hand much too quickly."

"I thought you were in the middle of a case. Can you leave at this point? And what about anything or 'anyone' else? Won't they object to you flying to help an old friend out of the blue?"

"One, the case is in capable hands with my team. Two, I don't have anything or 'anyone' that can or will object to me flying out to help an 'old' friend. Third, you're not that old, and four, I can't wait to see you. I mean, help you with this situation." He reassures me, with his kind words.

"Thank you. I appreciate it. I'll see you tomorrow, actually later today."

Time flies when you're in deep conversation and trying to relay all the essential details of this case—my case. It's long past midnight. I better get some sleep. Before I do, I'm double-checking the doors and windows, putting the pry bars behind the doors, and locking my bedroom door. And maybe, just maybe put my Walther PPK .380 by my bed. Nobody is getting in here without an invitation.

Chapter 7

Elephant in the Room

Waking up to the roar of thunder may be a prelude to a tumultuous day. I'm surprised that I slept peacefully and soundly. Maybe knowing the calvary is on its way has given me a sense of comfort and reassurance. Hopefully, it's not a false sense of security. My perspective has to shift into one of deliberate action and strategic thinking.

The aroma of fresh-brewed coffee is rapidly clearing the cobwebs and allowing me to look at the list of possible "framers" with a renewed perspective. The rain's insistent pounding on the window is washing away, clearing my focus on the situation.

What if it's not a local, maybe somebody from my past? Somebody who may have followed me from Los Angeles to Louisiana. How could I forget the main reason for leaving the job behind? For moving back home a year ago. Sure, there was the dreadful nature and stressful atmosphere of the work. But it was that last assignment—that drove me away after the physical injury and the death threats that followed the conviction of the attacker.

That's the elephant in the room, which I kept from Robert. At the time, he was on a covert assignment somewhere on a need-to-know basis, and I did not need to know. When it happened, I felt I could manage it. I was never one to play the victim card. When he got back, we were never the same. He blamed it on his work. I was too wrapped up in the drama of the situation to open up to him. Looking back, I let him take the blame for the dissolution of our relationship. If I accept his assistance on this mayhem, we must start on neutral ground—no skeletons in the closet or the Bayou.

I'll prepare for his arrival with an open heart and mind. I need to confide in him fully to be on the same page to solve DuBois's murder and clear myself.

***

Speaking of opening up--is it too early to open a bottle of wine and play hostess? It's been at least a year since I've seen Robert. When I left LA, we thought it best to keep our distance to allow our relationship to morph into whatever it was to become. We did talk on the phone from time to time. It was always polite and somewhat contrived. Hopefully, he will be here to help me—and I have no idea how I will react to seeing him again. Gosh, I'm so nervous—this is not me. It must be; I'm the only one here. I'm glad for TK and TC. When you have pets, you can have a full-blown conversation, and if anybody hears it, you can say you're just talking to your furry friends, and people will nod and acknowledge—cause everybody does it.

There he is. I see his silhouette through the frosted glass in the front door. He appears taller than I remember—how could that be? Maybe he seems more imposing because, currently, I feel emotionally underimposed. Steady girl, let him ring the doorbell; don't run to the door. Take a breath, and calm yourself. He is a friend and here to help, that's all.

The doorbell ringing triggers my legs into motion. Opening the door and seeing Robert standing there couldn't be more awkward. What to do, what to do? Shake hands? Friendly hug? Will someone do something? As if on cue. Robert puts his bag down and reaches for a hug, sporting a vibrant smile. Talk about disarming an individual. I forgot, or instead, I tried to forget how wonderful it felt to be in his arms. It is very comforting, and it's melting all the awkwardness away. Now, I think I can start our visit and the challenges ahead on an even more emotional plane.

"Please come in and make yourself comfortable. Can I get you something to drink? How about some iced tea?" I say, smiling and acting somewhat normal.

"Iced tea sounds great. How about this rain? Do you think it will help with the humidity? Let's see what else can we chit-chat about to make us feel a little more comfortable with the oddness of this situation?" Robert says, on the verge of laughter.

"You got me, this is weird, but we've always thrived on weird, didn't we? That is the nature of our chosen careers, and morbid humor is a must to survive the gruesomeness of our professions. I changed professions to a degree, but the morbid humor remains. It is handy when dealing with clients, especially eccentric brides and weddings. I'll catch you up with that in a bit. But before I dive in, I must tell you what happened in Los Angeles with the last case I worked on. It may have contributed to us falling from grace." I say as I sit on the couch and hand him his iced tea.

"I'm here to help you now. Whatever happened in LA, it's in the past, and there is no need to rehash it. I'm okay with that." He says while lightly tapping my hand resting on the couch.

"I'm afraid what happened then may be related to what's happening now. We must consider the past to navigate the present and guarantee my future freedom."

"Okay, I'm listening."

"I want you to know I didn't keep information from you to keep you in the dark but to keep the dark from creeping on you after you returned from your assignment. When you returned from that particular case, you were silent and reserved. I know you had your reasons and the nature of your job; I've always respected the privacy and secrecy you had to maintain. I thought it best to keep what happened to myself until you had the time to debrief and release the emotional baggage you were carrying. When I thought you might be ready to hear me out, it seemed too late to share. Now I must do."

His grey eyes transfix on me. It feels as if he is looking through into my soul. It would be great if he could read my thoughts and save me from relieving the painful experience. Unfortunately, it's not that easy.

"I'm here for you, I'm listening, and there is no judgment. I'm here to help—whatever it takes. You know I care. I always will." Robert says with a hint of a smile.

"I was on an assignment that appeared to be a patterned crime scene. It exhibited similarities to three other murders—it was starting to look like the work of a serial killer. The brutality of the assault on the body was beyond description. Even timeworn experienced detectives had difficulty maintaining their composure, and the newbies did not have the stomach for it. I drew from the anger that rose in me and the empathy for the victim to give me the calm to do my job and take the necessary pictures, hopefully leading to stopping further massacres."

Robert is listening and, I'm sure, visualizing some of the crime scenes he's visited in his career. It's something that cannot be unseen once you see it. I'm conflicted about how much is necessary to share without relieving the pain, the fear, and the aftermath.

Robert interjects as if reading my mind, "I know this is tough; you've gone through a horrendous experience, but you must dredge up every detail so we can compile the puzzle pieces that will clear you. -Let's try something. Please close your eyes, breathe, and place yourself on that day. You're an observer, removed from physical pain; you watch, and you report what you see, nothing more relax, and tell me what Jessica is doing. You're you, but you're separate enough that nothing can harm you. You're watching and telling; go on."

My skeptical part is not buying this, but his soothing, hypnotic voice is hard to fight. Relax and go with it, relax and be. I cannot discern what his words are or what my subconscious is directing me.

"I'm at the station, finishing uploading the photos to the case file. I have a gut feeling something is missing. I must go back to the scene. Now that the scene has been preserved and doesn't have the troops, I might find something to link these three cases together. Is it the work of a serial killer, or do we have a copycat? Either way, the killer must be stopped."

"Go on." I hear Robert say faintly and feel compelled to keep talking.

"On my way out, I tell Sherry, Detective Sherry Lowell, that I'll be stopping by the scene to take a closer look and may take some additional photos. She's a friend, so I'll call her later when I get home."

"You're doing great. Take a deep breath, and please continue." Robert's reassuring voice seems distant but encouraging.

"I arrived at the high-rise known as The Carlotta on the 10000 block of Wilshire Blvd. I drove up the semi-circular driveway and left my car in the temporary stall. I wasn't planning to stay long. By all appearances, it seemed normal and luxurious. I presented my credentials to the reception clerk and told him I was going to the 20th floor. There was no need to elaborate. He took notice of my photographer's bag and the lanyard around my neck, which clearly stated LAPD Forensics, and waved me towards the elevator. He handed me a pass card with a code. I needed the pass to access the express elevator that would take me directly to the penthouse. As the elevator doors opened, nothing seemed out of place. Some lights were left on, so everything looked beautiful, glamorous, and ordinary. Suppose you call a $20,000 plus rental per month apartment standard. Walking down the hall towards the bedroom, I hesitated to enter. I knew the victim had been removed, but the gruesome visual remained. I joined the scene and stayed put observing, looking for something, not knowing what I was searching for and at the same time knowing it would reveal itself. I started taking pictures from different angles, which I may have overlooked earlier. The artificial lighting magnified some of the objects in the room. I noticed one of the pictures was crooked. Behind the picture, I discovered the corner of a safe. I carefully stepped over the stained Moroccan rugs and the pools of blood that soaked into the hardwood floors. I questioned how I had missed the angle of the picture previously. If it were in that position, I would have noted it. I must capture this now and record that it has moved since the team was here. I noticed it was slightly open as I walked closer to the elusive safe. Now, it was getting interesting. As I approached, I couldn't help but admire the view. It was like a carpet of rhinestones in a sea of dark blue velvet. It was a magical panoramic view.

I heard a noise, something dragging behind me. Looking at the glass reflection, I saw a man about to strike. I moved out of the way, and he fell forward. With the agility of a trapeze artist, he stood up and came at me. He was big, and I was no match for my somewhat rusty self-defense skills. There were enough objects in the way to buy me enough time to say something. I put my hand up as if this would stop this Hulk. I asked, what are you doing here? I'm here in an official capacity, I'm LAPD forensics, and I didn't break in. The LAPD thing made him reconsider for a second or two.

I asked what he was doing there and if he knew the victim. He said—he was tying loose ends. As he said that, he unintentionally glanced at the safe. I knew I was in trouble. He launched at me with a murderer's hatred in his eyes. I knew this would be a fight to the death, and I wasn't ready to go. I don't recall much; it's blurry, his hands around my throat, and I'm gasping for air. I remembered some training to drop down and make myself as heavy as possible. He stumbled forward. I picked up the crystal-based lamp and swung it onto his head with what strength I had left. I fell forward, seeing stars and black dots as I slumped onto the glass and steel coffee table with my shoulder. The next thing I remember is breathing through an oxygen mask, the paramedics surrounding me, and looking up at Sherry."

"Take a cleansing breath, stay relaxed, and open your eyes when ready. Breathe and let go. You're awake, you're energized, you're well." Robert says in his tranquil tone.

"That was amazing. I feel so relaxed, like I took a nice hot bath or a well-deserved nap. So, tell me, did I spill the beans? Did you get me to talk?" I say, joking a bit and hoping I didn't say anything incriminating about my feelings for him. Yes, I just realized I may still have feelings, or maybe it's just nice to have a protector type around.

"Earth to Jessica, where were you just now?" He says, raising an eyebrow.

"Just coming in for a landing after that journey. Where did you learn to do that?"

"Part of the training, hypnosis, and NLP (Neuro-Linguistics Programming) is handy for interrogations. Sometimes, individuals are so tense they don't remember anything. With some hypnosis and relaxation techniques, we can get those fine details that may effectively catch the bad guys or gals. As far as NLP, it helps with the ability to ascertain if somebody is lying, nervous, or anxious by some of the body language or automatic physical responses. Tools of the trade."

How did I date this man for five years and not know all this fascinating stuff? We were both working long hours and needed more time for deep conversations. Plus, he tried not to bring home his work, and I did the same. That doesn't leave many conversations to share at the dinner table.

"I'm sorry you went through all that. You said you didn't feel like telling me when I returned from the three-month assignment, which I thought would never end. But I would hope that you would have shared it with me. Going through that ordeal alone must have been an enormous burden by yourself."

"I wasn't completely alone; I had my buddies at the department. Sherry is a great friend; she was there for me through the physical recovery, my shoulder surgery, and all the emotional ups and downs. This ordeal happened soon after you left, so by the time you got back—I had some time to get myself together and not need that much adult supervision." I tell him with a convincing smile. I don't want him to feel bad or pity me.

Back into his interrogation mode, "Why do you think there may be a connection to the frame up here in New Orleans?"

"Well, after I was found slightly unconscious but fortunately not dead, I saw the other guy was out like a light. He wasn't moving and had a big gash on his head. He lived, healed, was arrested, charged, and convicted. As far as I know, he is still serving time. He was the serial killer of at least three high society murders in and around LA, and there are still files full of circumstantial evidence that may link him to about ten or more victims. When I left, a couple of detectives were relentless at following any leads and resolved to open any cold cases that may be cross-referenced with the new advances in DNA discovery. He had committed these murders but had no arrest record for anything. He didn't have as much as a parking ticket; he was squeaky clean—so he didn't appear in law enforcement databases. When he was arrested at the apartment, his prints and DNA were everywhere, including under my nails. At that time, they had the DNA evidence to tie him to the other two murders and get his conviction and sentence." It's time to take a breath and a sip or two of tea.

"Okay, so you were undeniably responsible for his capture. I can see how he may blame you for his bad luck. According to him, he was innocent of any wrongdoing until he got caught. Poor fellow!" Robert says, shaking his head.

"A week after, he was sent to Pelican Bay State Prison up north, near the Oregon border. I started receiving calls in the middle of the night. The calls were not from prison, but it sounded like him. They started coming almost every night, sometimes several times at night. They were very threatening and descriptive. The description matched the MO of the crimes committed to the three serial killer victims. The person had information never released to the press, so it was deemed it was somebody on the outside but directly connected to him. Then, packages, dead flowers, and bugs started to arrive, and it got worse. Of course, I had the department take possession of the objects, and they examined them thoroughly but never found any identifying traits, fingerprints, or DNA—nothing traceable. We figured it might be a relative. Everybody living and with the remotest relation to him was questioned, interrogated, and pushed to talk as much as legally possible. Nobody broke. Nobody had anything nice to say about him. Perhaps that's why he turned out to be a serial killer—all the hate towards him, or maybe he was bad to the bone and deserved the disdain."

"And you didn't tell me all this, why?" He said with concern and anger in his eyes.

"Your job, more often than not, puts you in a life-or-death situation. The last thing you needed to hear from me was I just received another threat, or guess what I found at my door today, a dead snake. I couldn't do anything to jeopardize your cover or your safety. So, I dealt with it. I knew I confided with people who could protect me. Well, until one day when I received a bomb. It was a considerably basic one, and it didn't detonate because the battery had detached itself and was laying there unable to make contact."

"How was it that I didn't see any of this?" he says with a bewildered look.

"I thought they had somebody watching the house. When you came back, things stopped. When you traveled, they started again. So, I was afraid for your well-being. I wasn't myself when you were home, and things just fell apart. I cared too much to put you in danger. That's why I thought about moving away and coming here. It was the safest thing to do. Cutting ties and breaking up with you left you off the hook. Nobody would try to harm you to get to me." There it is in a nutshell—more like a whole can of nuts. I am exhausted, but I'm also relieved.

"Come here." He says with open arms. "You know two are better than one when solving mysteries, right?

Now, let's do some math together and solve this one. We'll keep each other safe and solve this mess. I have some ideas and people in this town who'll happily lend a hand."

Chapter 8

Hello, detective

Morning came much too early. I can't believe we fell asleep on the couch and recliner and never reached the bedroom. The glaring bright light jars my eyelids open—since I have no window coverings. The view from my front windows is much too gorgeous to block. I love watching the glimmering trees in the sunlight, and the waterfowl fly by without masking the beauty. Poetic, I know, right now, my eyeballs are burning. It's time to make coffee and hop in the shower. Today is going to be interesting, to say the least. Wow, there is sleeping beauty on the couch flanked by TC and TK. This sight is not exactly the picture of a super-agent man. I will not make fun of or take photos—after all, this man carries a gun.

I feel much better now. A refreshing, cool water shower does wonders for waking up, along with the smell of freshly brewed coffee.

"What a welcome sight!" I say while be-lining for the coffee cup, Robert is holding in my direction.

"Well, thanks...I haven't showered yet and am still wearing what I wore yesterday, minus the tie." Robert says, with a questionable look.

"No offense, I was talking about the coffee. Where are we going to go first? Whom do you know who can help us decipher this situation, and when can we get started? I have a few people in mind who I know didn't care for Antoine--we can talk to them first."

"Are you sure you didn't already have a coffee or two? How about I take a quick and much-needed shower, and then we make an action plan for the day?"

"So, we're going to be logical and strategic in this approach—great idea. I guess you can take the lead on this one." I say, chuckling. I can get overzealous sometimes, especially when my freedom and reputation are at stake.

He's right. It is best to approach the situation intentionally and methodically. I can't let my emotions get in the way. So, what do I wear that says—I'm logical and methodical? I'm afraid I don't have anything like that in my closet. I'll have to go with comfort cotton and confidence.

Well, here he is—sporting a casual look of jeans, a steel grey button-down shirt that brings out his eyes, and a light weave cotton sports jacket. He always wears a coat to conceal his shoulder holster.

"First, we'll head to the Police Department and talk with Detective LaCroix. We'll see if he's learned anything new and how he is following up on the case. Once we learn what he's up to or where he plans to go with the information gathered, we'll have something to go on. Based on that, we'll talk to your persons of interest."

After several phone calls, Robert tracks down the elusive Detective LaCroix.

"Let's do this!" I say, shifting the jeep in gear and backing up a little too quickly, scattering gravel all over the gardenias on the side of the driveway.

***

We're heading to the French Quarter to the NOLA Police Department sub-station on Royal Street. The downside to this place is the street parking. The upside is it's next to Café Beignet, the best coffee around, not to mention the flakey, fluffy, sweet, and delicious beignets. As we drive, searching for a precious parking spot, I can't help noticing the building's old, perhaps a little dilapidated but still grand exterior. The 'Doric' columns on the facade call attention, and the ones at the entrance let you know of the historical setting of yesteryear. I believe it was a bank at one time built around 1827. It also has an impressive black rod iron fence surrounding the building, though on most occasions, the gates remain open to the public.

We're entering the lobby area, and it strikes me funny; of course, I must share my thoughts; I'm transparent.

"They must have had a sale on columns when they built this place," I say, looking around amusingly.

Robert approaches the front desk and the sergeant on duty. Still chuckling, this has an adverse reaction from the sergeant, who takes his front desk duties and the eating of beignets behind the desk seriously. Robert ignores the white powder sugar on the sides of the sergeant's lips and tells him we're here to meet with Detective LaCroix.

"Is he expecting you?" He states while meeting Robert's gaze with disapproval.

"Yes, Sergeant, you can tell him Special Agent Hunt is here along with Ms. Martin," Robert says, seamlessly showing his ID.

"Yes, sir, I'll let him know straight away." The sergeant says, picking up the phone and straightening his posture slightly.

It's incredible what the badge of a Federal Agent does for people's demeanor. Let's hope we get the same reception and cooperation from the Detective.

Speaking of the Detective, he comes around the corner from what appears to be a false façade on a theater stage, but apparently, around the enormous reception desk are a few doors to individual offices.

"Follow me." He says curtly, leading us away toward the back of the room.

Robert and I exchange glances while following close behind as if we were wayward children on the way to the principal's office. This meeting shall be an exciting barter for information.

The Detective moves behind the desk and, as he sits, says have a seat. What, no Hello? What kind of Southern hospitality is this? I was raised here, and I know this is not it. He may have a lot on his mind. I'm willing to give him the benefit of the doubt.

Before sitting down, Robert extends his hand and formally introduces himself.

"Detective, I'm Agent Robert Hunt with the FBI. You can call me Robert. I'm here in an unofficial capacity.

As if being forced to act politely, the Detective shakes hands. Looking up briefly, he says. "You can call me Detective LaCroix. I'm the head detective on this case."

"Point taken, Detective," Robert states, unthreatened.

Well, well, well, this is different from how I imagined or wished for. Hopefully, once we get in the spirit of cooperation and exchange ideas, the Detective will realize we're on the same page.

"So, why are you here? Do you have any pertinent leads or information to this case?" Detective LaCroix says, straight to the point.

"We were hoping to have a dialogue to see what you have discovered so far and how it pertains to clearing any clouds over Ms. Martin's involvement or lack of involvement in this case. We're going to be speaking with people who we believe may have something to do with the situation—or may have some information that may be valuable to solve this and clear any misgivings towards Jessica--Ms. Martin. We're hoping that we can coordinate our efforts towards the common goal of solving this case as soon as possible."

"Like I said when I introduced myself, I'm the lead Detective on this case. I don't need any assistance from outsiders. I would rather you stay out of my investigation and let me see it through, no matter where it leads and who's found responsible for the murder of Mr. DuBois."

Ok, I've had enough of Detective LaCroix. This is my life we're talking about. I won't stand on the sidelines and have an uncaring individual take the reins and play Russian Roulette with the outcome.

"Detective, with all due respect. I cannot promise I will stand idly by and do nothing until it's too late for me to clear my name. I don't know why; I'm implicated in this situation. I have no clue why somebody would come into my house in the middle of the night and steal my walking stick to place it as incriminating evidence at the scene of a murder. But I can assure you—I will find the answers. When I do, I will communicate those to you." I say with absolute resolve.

"Let me give you a word of warning, Ms. Martin. Currently, you remain a person of interest. You interfere in my case and may escalate your standing and face additional charges, like interfering in a police investigation, obstruction of justice, or withholding evidence if you should find something and hesitate to keep me in the know. Are we clear?"

"Detective LaCroix, I'm as clear on this as the muddy waters of the Bayou. What I'm hearing is a threat, and I don't understand why you would object to any assistance in clearing this case. Unless you have some personal agenda to bury this one without ruffling too many feathers." I say, fighting fire with fire.

"I would tell your friend here to mind her manners and tread lightly." The Detective addresses Robert with a smirk full of condescension.

"Detective Louis LaCroix, it is you who should mind his manners. Threatening a person who wants to clear her name and aid you in your investigation by sharing information, she may obtain is not wise. Even more unwise is doing so in the presence of a veteran FBI Special Agent. I've been on diversified special details for 20 years and know most departments' internal functions. From what I hear from my sources, is that you could use our help. Numerous open cases under your command remain unsolved and have questionable outcomes. You wouldn't want me to come in officially to investigate those files, would you? Police work, like life, is about making the wisest choices. You have a choice: welcome our assistance so the right murderer is arrested as soon as possible or follow dead ends on your own and lose your gold shield. It's your choice. What is it going to be?" Robert says, drilling him with his cool steel gaze.

"I guess it can't hurt to have more eyes and ears on the case. But you will bring everything and anything you discover my way." He said, standing up and extending his hand for a handshake, first in my direction, respectfully addressing me as Ms. Martin, then shaking hands with Robert, addressing him as Agent Hunt.

Chapter 9

Nothing like a Beignet

"After that sour note, I need something sweet. Let's get a coffee and a much-needed beignet," I say as I drag Robert by the arm.

"Well, he is easy to please and work with. Fortunately, I've had my share of Detectives who want to work as Lone Wolves. They don't value that police work is about teamwork, not only with the law enforcement personnel but with all the resources that work together to gather the puzzle pieces and eventually solve the crime. This team extends to the civilians who get involved and provide information and the paid informants who are our eyes and ears on the streets. He is young. He'll learn as he works up the ranks, or screw up once too many times and end up in uniform if he's 'lucky' doing parking detail." Robert says.

"Oh no, you created an awful image I cannot unsee. Instead of the dapper suit and shiny shoes, he'll be wearing much too tight, short-leg pants over heavy-beat walking boots. It's not an image I want to entertain, but it's there, nonetheless. And for that, you're buying."

Snickering, he opens the door and waves me in. There, as if waiting for us, is a cute little table by the front window. The décor in this quaint and cozy place is like an outdoor Bistro café with small white rod-iron tables and chairs. As if reading my mind, as soon as the waitress comes to the table, Robert orders--Two beignets and two cafes au lait.

"You remember my favorite, midafternoon coffee, just enough caffeine to let you coast for the day and ease into the evening. Speaking of an evening look, who's walking in..."

Robert looks over my shoulder and sees the lady I'm referring to. He has a questionable look on his face.

"Am I supposed to know who she is?"

"No, not yet, but you will soon enough."

I'm getting up and catching up with her. It's been a while since I've seen her, and she was good friends with Antoine. I must offer my condolences and reconnect.

"Margo!" I say, tapping lightly on her shoulder.

She turns around, and her eyes open as big as saucers; her expression is surprise and goodwill.

"Mon Cher, how have you been? I have not seen you in way too long. What brings you to the Big Easy? She says without taking a single breath.

"I've been back for a while now.

"And you haven't come by to visit and have a drink to celebrate your homecoming? We'll have to fix that."

"I'd like you to meet someone, I say, motioning to Robert."

"Now, I know why you've been too busy to come by and have a drink with little ol' me...? Margo says while jokingly smacking me on the arm.

"Margo, this is my friend, Robert. He's going to be visiting for a while."

"Margo, it is a pleasure to meet you," Robert says, standing up and greeting her with his devastating smile. "Would you care to join us?"

"Oh my, how can I resist?"

The waitress is bringing our order already. Perfect timing.

"Margo, what will you have?" Robert asks graciously.

"I'll have the same as you two; it looks delicious, and I don't start my serious drinking till I get to work," Margo says with a wicked little laugh.

"Margo owns Margo's Hole in the Wall on Bourbon Street. It's a real down-home fun place. It's a great spot to hang out and let loose or relax, whatever you choose. We'll have to go there sometime."

"Well, thank you, Jessica. I would love to say you should see it now that I got it all renovated and jazzed up—but I haven't done a thing to the place since I bought it ten years ago, and that's just the way my people like it. The dingier, the better. Hey, I don't mean to intrude on the time and events you may have planned for the evening, but why don't you come by and have a few drinks, and let's get re-acquainted."

"It sounds like a plan," I say, looking at Robert and hopefully communicating this will be perfect to continue our covert investigation.

"We look forward to it. We'll come by later, for sure." Robert seals the deal.

There is no time like the present to address the elephant in the room. I'm having mixed emotions about how to bring about the conversation about Antoine. I had not seen Margo in a long time, but she was a good friend. Some would say a little more than friends with

Antoine. I don't want to come across as a nosy buddy, but it might be taken as insensitive if I don't mention it.

"Margo, I'm sure you heard about Antoine's unfortunate demise. I understand you were friends, so I'd like to offer my condolences to you." Time to set back and observe.

"Yes, I heard about it. We were friends on and off. He was a busy guy with all his crazy businesses and way too many visits to the Casino. I am sorry to hear about it, but I'm not surprised—he occasionally hung out with some shady characters. That's one of the reasons that kept us apart. I was scared for him. Sometimes, I was scared when some of his acquaintances would show up at the Hole. I don't need that kind of patron at my establishment. Hopefully, now they won't be coming around looking for him to settle one deal or another." Margo says, keeping her composure, betrayed by the wetness in her eyes. "Well, look at the time. I must be going and open up for the Happy Hour crowd. Of course, here in the Big Easy, everybody is happy all the time, am I right? Margo says as she gets up, hastily says thank you, and dashes off.

"Somehow, I feel that touched a nerve, but she's hard to read." Says Robert, sitting back and taking it all in.

"She's either grieving the heavy loss of her friend, or she knows a lot more than she's willing to say. I'm glad she didn't see your badge; it would have closed her off to further sharing."

"I keep it in my pocket unless I'm working a case. Right now, I'm just Joe Citizen, not Agent Hunt."

"Oh, so—should I have introduced you as "Joe"?" I say, laughing.

Looking down at the table, I realized Margo hardly touched her food or coffee.

"She must have been distraught. She took a few bites of the beignet and sipped her coffee before I mentioned Antoine. After that, she didn't eat or drink anymore. She's more troubled than she is willing to show. I wonder how deep her connection was. We need to go to her bar and follow up."

"I agree. It has to be an easy conversation. If Margo feels pushed, she'll clam up. She shows a fun and tough exterior, but I could sense she is at a breaking point."

Chapter 10

Time of Discovery

"So, where is Margo's Hole in the Wall? Is it within walking distance? I'd love to take in the ambiance of this city."

"Everything in the French Quarter is within walking distance. It all depends on how much you like walking and how much time you have on your hands—there is so much to see, hear, and be part of that it always takes longer than expected to get anywhere. Margo's place is only about three to four blocks from here near the corner of Bourbon Street and New Orleans Street." I say with knowledge of the lay of the land. "We're staying on Royal Street as long as possible; Bourbon is way too busy and gets a little too crowded for my taste, plus you always risk getting a drink or two spilled on you by tourists who love to walk around with their favorite local drinks called Hurricanes."

"Hurricanes? Interesting, that is considered a good thing around here?

"They're tasty and refreshing, but if not sipped slowly and if you drink them on an empty stomach, you can feel like you've been through one, not knowing where you are or what hit you—the thing is they're delicious, sweet and delightful," I say as a true connoisseur, yes, I've had my share like I say they're delightful-especially if consumed in moderation.

"I'm curious what's in them?"

"I'm no expert, but I believe this is what goes in them. Light rum, dark rum, passion fruit juice, orange juice, lime juice, syrup, grenadine—and let's not forget to garnish with an Orange Slice and a Cherry. Of course, the ratio of the ingredients can make it from a category 1 to a full category 5—I would not recommend anything above a 2." I say, laughing and perhaps remembering personal experiences with the highly appraised local beverage.

"You intrigued me; I'll have to try one when this situation ends. Until then, I'll stick to beer. I must always have my senses sharp. So, don't give me a funny look if I order a Root Beer." Robert says, laughing.

"I'm already missing Antoine; he was a good man. I know it seems he had a colorful past and perhaps some hidden secrets which may have made him vulnerable to the criminal element in this city—but to me, he has always been fair, kind, and a great resource for my income. He was the first to offer me a job as a photographer for all his marketing, flyers, website, and anything else he could dream up in his entrepreneurial mind." I say, trying not to let my sentiments get to me.

Sensing my sudden silence as a sign I am getting emotional, Robert puts an arm over my shoulder and says, "It's okay to feel, and healthy not to bottle it up. You haven't had the opportunity to grieve at your own pace. Knowing somebody you know was murdered is shocking enough without the alleged accusation or involvement in the crime.

Nothing we do will bring him back, but we can do our best to solve this and find him justice."

It's interesting to have this conversation as we walk by the Law Library of Louisiana and the Appeals Court. There may be a positive message: the Law will be on our side or at least to the right of us as we walk on by.

I take a deep breath and clear my head. Emotions get in the way of clear thinking, which is what I need. Of course, taking a deep breath near the multitude of restaurants can be an attack on the olfactory system. Right now, all I can smell is the savory scent of French Onion Soup, wafting from the Royal House Oyster Bar across the street.

"How can you walk down the street and not stop at every restaurant; it smells so inviting?"

"Well, I can give you three reasons. One, some of these restaurants are pretty pricey. Two, if you stopped and ate that often, you would be four hundred pounds in no time. Third, you get used to it after a while. We have Creole Cooking at its best. You can have it any day of the week. And if you want to lose your appetite, all you have to do is walk a block up to Bourbon Street a few hours after sundown, and the smells coming from the street will completely cure you of food cravings."

"Just the thought of that has cured me of any hunger I may have for a while; thanks a lot," Robert says mockingly.

"Okay, enough distractions. We need a plan, so Margo doesn't suspect us of suspecting her. We need to delve deeper into how serious her relationship with Antoine was." I'm getting back into saving my behind mode.

"I feel the fact that he was a gambler and perhaps not a good one may also have something to do with his unfortunate demise." Especially if he owed the wrong people money, and they all fall under the wrong people description when you cannot get a legit loan from a bank."

I point to a charming entryway in a storefront. "This 'was' DuBois' main office for Nola's Tourist Tours. I thought it was closed, but it looks like there is somebody inside. Let's check it out." I say without hesitation.

I open the door and adjust my eyes to the dim light inside. I remember Antoine had an assistant but had gone to Paris for a month. Who could be in the back room?

"Hello, anybody back there?" says Robert with authority.

"Yes, I'm coming. Just hold on a minute—I'll be right out."

"That sounds like Thomas, Antoine's assistant, but he wasn't supposed to be in town. Unless somebody told him about Antoine, and he flew back to take care of things."

"Well, Hi! How are you, Jessica? And who may this be? Oh, where are my manners? Let me introduce myself. I'm Thomas Dupris, and I'm Antoine's right-hand man. Well, I was, I guess—I'm all hands-on deck now." He says with a nervous chuckle and moist eyes."

"I thought you went to Paris for a month or so. When did you get back?" I say, breaking up the awkward moment.

"There was a change of plans, and I didn't go. As always, Antoine overbooked himself and everybody else, and there was never time for anything else but work. I loved the man, but he wanted way too much from everybody to keep up with his expenses or gambling debts. I shouldn't speak ill of the dead, especially in this town, but he drove everybody nuts. He was running his business into the ground by not giving the kind of care people deserve. He didn't care about the conflicting bookings; he didn't care if the equipment wasn't up to par and repaired like the boats and the hovercrafts on the bayou. Everything needs downtime for repair and safety—he didn't care. He wanted everything running around the clock without regard for the safety or the well-being of the people working for him. After a while, this may drive people to do things they would never think of doing in a sane world, but Antoine's world was not sane. His world was dragging everybody around him down, and some people cannot be dragged under."

"Do you know anybody who may have been mad enough to kill Antoine?" Roberts asks.

"Where do I begin? There are so many. You see, he owned a piece of everything that had anything to do with the tours in the city, out of the city, and in the bayou surrounding the city. All the different Tour offices you see around town are like a franchisee. Antoine would help them set up the business and then take a cut. Lately, he's been upping the fees and taking larger cuts, which would make people angry."

"Angry enough to kill?"

Chapter 11

No Upper Hand

"I think Thomas just opened Pandora's box with that statement. It is a good thing we left when we did. We don't want to come in too strong with the questions. People tend to clam up and panic. We've established a rapport; he doesn't know I'm police, and he doesn't need to know at this point. Just here as a friend. Next time we meet, he'll have his guard down and perhaps his emotions in check. Then it will be timely to ask for a list of persons of interest who may have had it in for DuBois."

***

"Here we are at Margo's Famous Hole in the Wall," I say, waving my hand grandly.

"If this place is so famous, how come I've never heard of it?" Robert says, smirking away.

"Easy, you're not a local," I say, jabbing him lightly in the ribs. The ease of our relationship is returning, something I can use now. Having him here for support without judgment is the best thing to happen. Well, the best thing would be not to be in the middle of a homicide investigation. Oh well, we must take the good with the bad. With his help, I'm sure everything will be okay. I will never lose hope. It's not in my nature. I navigate my thoughts out of the gloom of the circumstances as I navigate the path to a clear booth in the dimness of this place with Robert at my six.

"Jessica!" Margo is shouting across the room. She should be an opera singer. I heard her above the noisy crowd and the band tuning their instruments for their first set.

"Jessica, Robert, over here—I saved you a table. I knew you'd come. At least, I was hoping you would."

"Thank you, Margo, this is perfect," Robert says as he inspects the location. The booth gives a clear panorama of the place, a step above the rest of the floor. There is a good view of the front door, and it is close enough to the back of the place, just in case a fast getaway is needed. Not to mention a clear sight of the band without having speakers above our heads.

"So, what will you have? We just got this Absinthe called Lucid from France; it is to die for. You must try it..." Margo offers over-enthusiastically.

"I think we're going to start with a couple of Abitas. Do you have 'The Boot'?" I ask, showing off a little Louisiana pride. The Boot brand of Abita's beer is only sold in Louisiana. Of course, other flavors of Abita's are sold throughout.

"I take it that's not Root beer. Robert says, shaking his head.

"No, it is not, but remember you're not at work. This situation is tense, and we could both use a little relaxation. I'm sure at 6'3", you can handle one or two beers. After all, if you come to the bar to ask questions and don't partake, your cover may be blown.

"You're right. I just wished this could be behind us, and we would be drinking to celebrate, not to prepare for the unknown journey ahead." He said without hiding his concern.

Here comes Margo, carrying three 'Boots,' I guess she's joining us. Perfect, this is just what we were going for. Casual conversation and deep analysis of what is her truth.

"I'm glad to see you're joining us."

"One of the few perks of owning this joint is I get to take breaks whenever I feel like it, or when I'm not needed, or breaking up—so-called disagreements with some unruly patrons who don't know their limits. That is always fun."

"When 'disagreements' get physical, you have bouncers take care of things, don't you?" Robert asks.

"With a couple of tours overseas before I returned and opened this place. I'm more than capable of taking care of myself. I can swing a club with the best of them. This bar is my place; I don't let anybody take advantage because it's a woman-owned business. I have bouncers, and they have my back, but I demand respect, and I get it. Nobody gets the upper hand or asks for more than they deserve. If they do, things can get ugly. It's the only way to survive here in the so-called Big Easy."

Robert and I exchange glances as we both think the same thing, I'm sure. The band starts playing, and the noise level goes through the roof. There is no way we will continue a civil conversation under these conditions. Margo is looking a little distant suddenly. It's almost like she caught herself sharing a little too much.

"I must get back to the grind. The beers are on the house." She says as she moves too quickly to give us a chance to answer. We can only smile and wave as she disappears into the crowd and towards the bar.

"Well, that was a sudden dismissal. By saying the beers are on the house, I'm interpreting it as saying, drink up and get out. Or am I reading too much into it?

"There was a shift in her demeanor. I'll leave a twenty on the table. I don't want to owe her any favors. She seems capable of a lot, but could she be capable of murder?

Chapter 12

Meeting of the Minds and Hearts

"Let's make our way back to the car via Jackson Square. We passed the back of it on the way here. It is something to see after dark. The Gothic architecture takes you back. It's as if you're transported in time." I say, feeling like I want to escape from the seriousness of the circumstances.

"Maybe, if we're carried back in time, we could prevent poor Antoine from getting killed, and you wouldn't be in the middle of this."

"We can only wish. I need to suspend reality for a few moments. My head is reeling with ideas, suspects, and, more than anything, too many unanswered questions." I say, feeling a little discouraged.

We're walking in silence, lost in our thoughts, while the world around us explodes with the sound of life, laughter, and music.

I see a welcome sight as we turn on Saint Ann Street from Royal Street: my friend Rene and her cousin Cecilia Rogers. Cecilia happens to be a Pathologist at the Sheriff's Department Morgue. They're strolling in our walking direction, so we must catch up. My energy heightens, and I can hardly contain myself from rushing them and drilling Cecilia for answers. I must restrain myself, and I'm sure after the introductions, Robert will know precisely how to lead the conversation and get some much-needed answers.

"Rene, Cecilia!" I call out.

"Oh my Gosh! We were talking about you." Rene says.

"Good things, I hope."

"Always good things about you, but not so good about the circumstances."

"Rene, you remember Robert. And this is Cecilia Rene's cousin." I say, ensuring I don't neglect the customary social graces in my rush to find answers.

Robert smiles and says, "Hi, Rene, long time no see. And Cecilia, I didn't know you were related to Rene. It's a pleasure to see you again."

"You know each other?" I say, a bit surprised and making sure my curiosity is not misinterpreted as anything else.

"Cecilia was most influential in capturing a notorious serial killer that the FBI had been tracking across a few southern states. It was her forensic expertise and insight which led to the apprehension and imprisonment of the suspect."

"Small world, isn't it?" I say with an admittedly unnoticed sigh of relief.

"Shall we walk for a bit and catch up?" Rene says as if reading my mind.

"Sure, now where do we begin? That is the question. There is so much going on, and I'm in the dark about why I'm in the middle."

Cecilia, who's been silent up to this point, seems a little edgy, as if she has something to share but does not know where to start or what to divulge. Robert and I exchanged looks. We both notice her uncertainty and uneasiness.

Robert makes the move and asks. "I know there are certain things that you may feel uncomfortable sharing at this time of the investigation. You don't want to share information that may jeopardize your position—but is there something we need to know? Something which could help us clear Jessica. We can be discreet with any information you provide."

Cecilia breathes as if the release valve has opened; now, she is free to speak. "The preliminary results of the autopsy showed the obvious blunt force trauma to the back of the head. After a more thorough examination, the toxicology report revealed unusual and non-descript traces of unknown origin. Perhaps Dubois was forced to consume a poison or toxic substance. We're still analyzing the properties to find the source of the matter in question. In conclusion, the trauma to the head was post-mortem."

"Post-mortem?" Robert echoed. "You mean he was hit on the head after death—as a cover-up. That is most interesting and the key to this Pandora's box. If we can discern the poison, we can discover who may have access to such a toxin. Once we have the 'What,' we can go for the 'Who,' and learn the 'Why.'

"Well, let's not forget the 'Where.' There were drag marks along the edge of the marsh. DuBois was murdered somewhere else and then taken to the Bayou. The closest access to that area is by airboat. There are walking trails to that point, but not driving ones. It wouldn't seem logical to drive, park in the parking areas, and carry the body to the location. We can start the 'Who' done it by finding out who owns their airboat in the Crescent City or vicinity. I doubt you could go to a fan boat rental place with a body in tow and not raise suspicion. Most reputable airboat enterprises operate during daylight hours for safety reasons. If somebody borrowed or stole a boat after hours, it would have been noted or caught on security cameras." I say, surprised at my deduction under stress.

"I hope you can keep this information confidential at this time. I mentioned it because Jessica, you're a friend, and you, Robert, are a top investigator. If anybody can solve this, my bet is on you. Some egos in places may block discovery if they do not follow procedures that benefit their advancement. If you know what I mean." Cecilia said with a friendly wink.

"Before you go, let me give you the number of a friend at the Louisiana Department of Wildlife and Fisheries. Her name is Yvon Batiste. She'll be able to provide the information of anyone who owns an airboat. They must be registered to operate in compliance with all city, parish, state, and federal laws. There are strict regulations like you cannot operate an airboat between the period beginning one hour after sunset and ending at sunrise. If somebody does, it draws attention, and maybe somebody reported it." Cecilia says.

"To evade observation, this person, who may own their airboat, would live near the marshlands. And would have access within minutes to avoid unwanted detection. I'm thinking out loud, aren't I?" I say, blushing a bit.

"Thanks, ladies, for your help, but most of all for having Jessica's back. I appreciate that." Robert says, putting his arm around my shoulder. "Now, let's get home safe and get a good night's rest. Looks like we have our work cut out for us." Robert adds.

Chapter 13

Mournful over Murder

Awoken once again by the sweet aroma of freshly brewed chicory coffee, I drag my legs over the edge of the bed. Still groggy from battling with blankets and pillows all night, I think they won. I was unable to get comfortable and had my mind racing without being near the finish line. I wish I could go to sleep and wake up realizing this was all a bad dream, and I could go back to taking pictures for Antoine and hearing his little chuckle when he would have some internal joke rambling through his head. He was funny that way. I still can't believe he could be involved in any wrongdoing. He was always sweet, helpful, courteous, and funny to me. I guess you never know people ultimately. He must have had a darker side, which drew in undesirable associations. One of those associations was destructive enough to kill. I must focus on that today and not lose sight of the goal: clearing myself and finding the murderer.

"I see you're dressed and ready to go. Want the coffee on a to-go cup, or should we take a moment and plan things out?" Robert says.

"To go cup is great. Thank you."

"I already called Officer Yvon Batiste and introduced myself. She'll be there waiting for us with whatever information she can provide."

"Officer Batiste, I thought in the Louisiana Department of Wildlife and Fisheries, they're called Wardens or Environmental Technicians," I say, showing off my knowledge of local enforcement.

"Well, Environmental Technician is a bit long of a title, and the word 'Warden' is not one I would think you want to get too comfortable with at this time."

"Very funny, for that remark...you drive," I say, throwing Robert the keys.

"You know that's not a punishment. I love to drive—tell me where to go, let me rephrase that, give me directions or the address, and I'll get us there.

"It's on Lakeshore Drive, past the New Orleans Police Crime Lab—you know where that is, don't you?"

"I do, and we're taking the scenic route by the lake instead of the 10 if that's okay?"

"You're driving; you're in charge—I have enough to think about," I say, briefly closing my eyes and taking a few deep breaths.

***

"This is a sterile-looking building. It seems sturdy and able to withstand on its own against the most inclement weather. Gives a sense of no-nonsense and thorough archive-keeping potential, but it lacks...'je ne sais quoi.'"

"I believe that's pretty much the function of this place. Practical office record keeping and document gathering efficiency, at least, I hope. I don't think architectural flourish and esthetics were part of the design. Mainly a practical building for practical purposes. I know it doesn't appeal to your sense of conceptual beauty. You look at everything as if you're looking through the eyes of the lens."

"It is that critical eye that allows no detail to go undetected--pretty good advantage in my line of work, wouldn't you say?" I say snickering.

"Okay, Eagle Eye, let's see what we can observe and how much information we can gather to keep you from being caged." Says with a friendly wink as he holds the door open for me.

The front doors give way to another set of doors. These are locked, and one must buzz to gain entrance. Robert places his badge and ID on the glass, and there is an immediate click in the door lock, giving us admittance. We proceed to the desk occupied by a uniformed young lady who is all smiles. She appears in great contrast to the austere atmosphere of the facility.

"Good morning. We're here to see Officer Yvon Batiste; she's expecting us."

"And you are? I know you have the FBI badge and all, but I have to write down who comes and goes in this building, you understand?"

"Of course, I'm Special Agent Robert Hunt, and this is my... associate Jessica Martin."

"Thank you. I'll let Warden Batiste know you're here." She says graciously, while not losing her bright smile for a second.

"Did she have to say 'Warden'? All of a sudden, I need air."

"Here she is. Remember, she's here to help us, so relax," Robert says as he pats my back discreetly.

It isn't hard to relax the moment I see Yvon. She competes with the front desk girl for the most charming smile.

"Come back to my office, you two. Can I get you some coffee, water, anything?"

The usual answer is, 'No, thank you, we're good,' but this is not the typical situation. So far, it feels like an invitation to someone's home, and it would be impolite to refuse the hospitality.

"Water will be great," I say.

"Make that two," Robert adds.

"Coming right up!" she says, reaching into the small refrigerator behind her desk and bringing out two Kentwood water bottles.

I take one long sip; my mouth is parched. This situation feels overly official, one of the many more I may face before I can clear myself of wrongdoing. I don't know why the reality and seriousness of the situation are hitting me so hard. I feel like drowning, yet I can't get enough water.

"After we spoke this morning, I went right to the registration records for owners and operators of airboats, hovercrafts, and the like in the immediate area within 15 miles of Bayou Savage. Here is a list of names and addresses. I hope this will help. Cecilia has briefed me on the urgency of the matter. We go way back, and a friend of Cecilia's or Rene's is a friend of mine. I'm here to help with anything you need. I want you to know that. Keep this list close to the vest; as they say, providing this information without a warrant can cost me my job." Yvon says as she hands me a manilla envelope with the list. I quickly put it inside my side bag. That way, nobody sees anything leaving the premises.

And now, I'm about to cry. It must be all the water I drank; it can't be that I feel overwhelmed and emotional. Jessica doesn't do emotional.

Chapter 14

The List

Walking back to the jeep, I pat the side of my satchel as if it held a treasure map leading to the most incredible fortune: my assured freedom. I feel like I'm founding an army of well-meaning and influential friends who have my back. This knowing relieves me, but I know better than to be overly confident. This investigative journey is just the beginning. One lead, one theory, there will be many avenues to explore—no exploring on an empty stomach.

"I could kill for a Shrimp Po'boy," I say, looking up at Robert.

"Interesting choice of words."

"I'm starving, and I was so excited about getting out of the house and making progress on the case; all I had was coffee."

"Okay, so where are the best Po'boys in town?"

"That depends, especially if you're craving shrimp."

"Shrimp sounds good to me."

"If you like the typical fried shrimp, Po'boy, we can go to Johnny's. But, if you want seared shrimp instead, there is none other than Killer Po'boys." I say with experience and knowledge of the casual local cuisine.

"Killers, it is—no offense," Robert says laughingly.

"Very funny. If it weren't for my morbid sense of humor, I could take offense, but no such thing. I think it is appropriate since we'll review the list and a possible lead to the killer.

It's about fifteen minutes away, not sure if they open at ten or eleven, so we have some time to--well, you know, walk around a bit."

"Aren't you anxious about looking at the list and seeing if there is a name that jumps out, somebody you may know or have a connection to both you and DuBois?"

"I'm afraid to look at it and find that there is no connection, and we're no closer to finding the murdered. It seems strange, but there are short moments where I feel we won't find the killer, and I'll spend the rest of my days in jail. It wouldn't be the first time an innocent person is sentenced for a crime they didn't commit. Fortunately, those moments don't last long, and I can shift into survivor mode—which gets me on track pretty quickly."

"I'm glad to hear that because we will find who did this, I promise."

"You know, rule number one, never promise the outcome of a case. There are too many variants."

"All the variants in the world will not keep me from clearing and protecting you; that is a solid promise. Some rules are made to be broken, and this is one of them." Robert says, with his steady gaze into my soul.

***

"I'm glad we got here before the lunch rush. Thus, getting a perfect seat by the window." I say, looking around and taking in the flavorful aroma of fresh spices.

"Okay, we got our food, got a great table. So, how long till you get the list out of the bag and start checking it out? I know you're hesitating because you're afraid it may be a dead-end. But remember, each closed lead is one step closer to another avenue of discovery. Let's take the first step—shall we?"

"You're right. Let's do this," I say, pulling the list out of my bag and taking a deep breath.

We inch closer to each other to share the view of the list. Robert puts his arm around my shoulder, making our seating arrangement less awkward and more comfortable.

"This is nice; the list is in alphabetical order. I don't recognize anybody on the A's or the B's. Let's see about the C's: Cabot, Caine..."

"Caine—May have to double check his name has a bit of a bad reputation," Robert says, interjecting a bit of humor.

"Should I continue? I ask as I put the list down for a moment to take a bite of my delicious Po'boy.

"Carradine, Carriveau, --Carron, Constantine !" Augh! I am gasping for air; my eyes are watering, and I can't catch my breath. I'm choking. Little black dots are floating about. A pounding in the middle of my shoulder blades liberates a piece of shrimp that goes flying across the room. Air gushing into my lungs, I'm not dead.

"Have some water and take small breaths; you're alright," Robert says as he steadies me back on the chair.

Mike, one of the cooks, asks if I'm okay if there is anything he can do or bring. The poor guy is panicked, but there is nothing he can do or did, for that matter, to cause my choking incident. It was all me.

"She'll be fine, and don't worry; she'll keep returning for your Po'boys- they're her favorite. Nothing will keep her away from this place. Just a case of a shrimp taking the wrong trajectory on the way down," Robert tells Mike with a reassuring smile.

"So, what did you see on the list which got you all choked up? —what too soon?"

"Way too soon," I say, laughing and shaking away the embarrassment.

"Constantine Carron owns a very exclusive Apothecary; he prides himself in importing the most unique and exotic plants from all over the world. He has a fabulous garden. Carron uses herbs and botanicals to make salves, tinctures, and teas. He claims he can make medical-grade cures for whatever ills you. He is a certified herbalist who claims he studied abroad in India, Indonesia, South America, Africa, and even Bulgaria. I remember him saying as if that was supposed to impress me. He is licensed to bring samples into the country and make his hybrids. It's all fascinating."

"You said, he said it as if trying to impress you? What was that about?"

"Well, he is the type who is confident, intelligent, and has worldly knowledge, which makes him think he can captivate any female he wants. I see through his façade and feel his narcissistic character overpower his impressive qualities. He has repeatedly asked me to have dinner with him on several occasions. He also invited me to his house, which is close to mine. It disturbed me when he mentioned that his house was only a few minutes from mine. This comment made me think he may have followed me home or did some digging to find my address. I have all my mail, car registration, and documentation addressed to a P.O. Box for security reasons. So, when he said that, it made me question his integrity, and I kept my distance from him intentionally."

"When was the last time you saw him?"

"A couple of weeks ago. Carron showed up at my door uninvited. He had an exotic plant he had just gotten from Asia, Africa, or the Amazon—I know it started with an A. It was gorgeous. I have never seen anything like it. He must have seen the look of wonder on my face. The next thing I knew, he was in my living room. I knew it wouldn't end well when he brought his other hand forward and held a bottle of wine. He commented about being a vintage wine to be consumed on special occasions. So, I took the bottle into the kitchen and put it in my wine rack. He then asked me to come over and look at some mockup drawings of some of his products and wanted to know if I could photographically reproduce the pictures. I sat for a minute to examine the drawings, and that's when he scooted closer to me. I immediately got up from the couch and told him it was getting late. I also mentioned that the next time he thought of dropping by, call first. He got up and walked towards the kitchen. He asked about the wine. I thanked him and told him I would keep it for a special occasion. He made a face but did not want to admit the apparent rejection. He then noticed my walking stick and asked about it. I told him it was given to me by my uncle, who was an artist. He carved it, especially for me. It was one of a kind. I never went hiking without it. He asked if he could take a closer look. I said okay since he was walking nearer to the door. He admired it and put it back in the corner behind the door. He gave a humble smile, a slight bow, and away he went.

It felt uncomfortable, but he left. I made a note never to let him enter my home again. There was something off outside of the work environment. Yet again, I wanted to make it clear that it was strictly a professional relationship, and it would never be anything else.

Did you see him after that?

"Last time I saw him, he heatedly argued with Antoine. I went to NOLA's Tourist Tours to give Antoine pictures I had taken for him, and I walked into the scene. Antoine seemed like he didn't have the strength to argue anymore. He kept asking Constantine to leave his shop but wouldn't budge. Constantine said -- this has to be settled, one way or another. I thought Antoine would have an episode of sorts; he was so pale. I stepped in and told Constantine to get out. I may have shoved him slightly—but he left. Antoine was so relieved that Constantine was gone he hugged me to thank me. The last I saw of Constantine was him staring through the glass door with the most hateful look."

"Do you recall when this took place?" Robert questions.

"I think a week or so before I found Antoine in the Bayou, I could be more precise when I check my planner—you know me, I write everything down."

"Do you think Constantine misconstrued your relationship with Antoine as more than a business friendship, and he might have acted on jealousy?"

"I don't know. I felt Constantine was strange and even creepy, but I didn't think he'd be the type to explode in a jealous rage. After seeing how he yelled at Antoine, anything is possible.

"Did you hear what they were arguing about before you step into the store?"

"I was on the phone with Rene as I walked into the place and hung up as I entered. So, I wasn't paying complete attention till I was in the midst of the argument, and at that point, all I heard were the threats."

"You heard Constantine threaten Antoine, and a week or so later, Antoine is found dead. I don't think we can dismiss those as idle threats. Constantine just placed himself on top of the list."

Chapter 15

Lies and Deceit

"We must immediately take the information about Constantine and his possible motive to Detective LaCroix. Let's go and see if we can catch him at the sub-station; we're minutes away, walking distance," Robert says.

"You're right, but let's call first; I don't feel we're on the buddy system of drop-by anytime with the Detective. Even though he said to bring him whatever we discovered, he said it reluctantly at best."

"Let's call him and let him know we're coming over with relevant information."

We're in luck. As we reach Royal Street, we see Detective LaCroix exiting his car and heading to the station.

At this distance, we should have excellent cell reception. Robert dials the Detective's mobile number.

"Detective Lacroix, this is Agent Hunt. We have some relevant information to share with you on the DuBois case."

"Oh yes, I'd love to chat, but I'm currently away from the station on another case, and I have no idea when I'll be heading back in. So, why don't I call you back when I have some free time."

"Detective Lacroix, I thought you agreed to cooperate with us in any way possible to clear Ms. Martin in this frame-up, so why would you blatantly lie to me about your whereabouts?"

"What do you mean?"

"We were approaching the station as you exited your vehicle and walked in. You were loosening your tie as if you would be in for a while and tackling some paperwork. So, Detective LaCroix, why the hesitation in speaking with us? Let me remind you that lying to an FBI agent has consequences, the least being obstruction of justice in an ongoing investigation. Just let the front desk know we're here to see you and you're expecting us. We're in the lobby."

As we approach the front desk, the officer points toward LaCroix's office. He is standing by his door with his hands on his hips, with the look on his face TC gets when she gets caught eating something she shouldn't and tries to blame it on the dog.

Walking into his office, it feels like the tables have turned.

"Detective LaCroix, you better take a seat. This information is significant to the case and might take a while."

"Well, I don't have much time; like I said, I'm working on a case."

"Let me refresh your memory. You said you were not working on another case at the station. We both know that was a stretch, so let's start fresh and give us your undivided attention. Let us know if you're no longer the lead Detective on this case. If you have been relieved, we'll be delighted to speak to the Detective in charge."

"I can assure you I'm still the lead Detective on this case. I apologize for the misunderstanding. Now, what is so important?" Says while letting out a breath as if releasing steam on a tea kettle.

After witnessing the incredible show of force between two men, I'm taking a moment to get my thoughts in order. I must admit that Robert showed dedication, control, and the definite upper hand in this short debate. I'm glad he is in my corner.

I recount the events of the confrontation with Constantine Carron and Antoine DuBois at the Nola Tourist Tours on the evening of August 1, a week and a day from when Dubois was discovered motionless in the marsh. I'm making sure to recall as much as I can from what I heard without adding anything that may be perceived as conjecture. As they say, only the facts.

"Are you going to write any of this information down?" I ask.

"I just wanted to listen to the story, and then I'll write down whatever I consider relevant. So far, it's hearsay and perhaps a vengeful way to point fault away from you. And, of course, avoid charges."

"Charges, have there been any formal charges made in the case," Robert asks.

"Well, not exactly, not yet, but it's just a matter of time," LaCroix states, leaning back on his chair as if he's done his job and he is done with us.

He adds, "You are not bringing me any concrete evidence. I can take nothing to anyone as a clear and complete resolution of the events. What am I supposed to do with this? Track down Mr. Carron and ask him if he threatened Mr. DuBois and if he carried through and settled things with Mr. DuBois permanently?"

"You can start by checking the whereabouts of Mr. Carron on the night before Mr. DuBois's body was found. Also, find out where he keeps his airboat. These are elementary questions with the education and experience of a rookie foot cop fresh out of the academy. So, what's keeping you from doing your job? You leave us no choice." Robert says, getting up from his chair.

***

"It's obvious; he is not lifting a finger to clear me on this. What is his deal? Never met him before. Therefore, he has no reason to hate me or want to see me go to the Grey Bar Hotel."

"You say that as if he knew you, he would have a reason to hate you—I don't think that would be the case," Robert says lightheartedly.

"Alright, we're on our own on this one. We need to get some evidence on Carron. Let's do it tonight. First, we'll swing by Carron's Apothecary and Botanicals on Toulouse Street."

"We're going by his shop. What do you have in mind?"

"I want to walk in casually and get a read on him. I'll say you're a friend from out of town, and you can't shake a headache. We're just shopping for one of his famous botanical remedies or teas. I want him to think I'm unaware of his possible involvement."

"That's a good start. Are you sure you've never worked undercover? He is a plausible suspect, but why would he want to frame you?"

"Maybe he thinks I overheard more of the conversation than I did. Self-preservation: he frames me before I go to the police and tell them about his threats. As you heard, Det. LaCroix stated I may be bringing information against Carron to detract attention from me. My thoughts and opinions don't carry much weight right now—unless we find conclusive evidence to tie Carron to DuBois. It's just a theory at this time, and we have to start somewhere. I know he's involved; I feel it in my gut."

Chapter 16

The Apothecary

W e're here at Constantine Carron's Apothecary." I say, walking into the shop, which never ceases to amaze me. "This place makes me feel like a kid in a candy store. It is full of teas, plants, and some so-called cure-alls from all over the world. It fascinates me and fills me with wonder. It carries strange and esoteric energy. A mysterious combination of healing and powerful toxins which, if not used in the precise measures, could be lethal."

"You're not kidding; this place is packed with international goods. It is remarkable how the shelves have little flags as to where the products come from. And where is our illustrious shopkeeper? Perhaps, in the back laboratory, making a new concoction for some unsuspecting soul." Robert whispers.

"Unfortunately, that may not be far-fetched," I whispered back.

We're moving towards the back of the store in silence, still with no sign of Constantine. Suddenly, he pops up from behind the cash register without missing a beat. He belts out his welcome slogan. "Welcome to Constantine's Apothecary, Botanicals, and International Exotic Teas and Elixirs. How may I be of service?"

"Good afternoon, Constantine. I was showing my friend around town, and he's developed a headache. Is there anything you can suggest? —he doesn't do Pharma." I say to break the ice and as a reason for stopping by without arousing suspicion. This fellow is cunning and not to be underestimated.

"Is it a throbbing type of pain, just in the temples? Can you describe the symptoms to me?" He says, looking over his glasses.

"I'm feeling pressure on the front of my head and perhaps a little going down my sinuses," Robert says as he squints his eyes and scrunches his nose.

Robert is so believable in his description that I'm thinking, poor guy, headache and all, and he is so accommodating. Of course, I realize this is part of the story, and he's playing his role perfectly.

"I have exactly what you need. This Eucalyptus essential oil from the Land Down Under will do the trick. Here, put a drop or two on this tissue and inhale lightly. Your headache will disappear within minutes--if that's all that ails you." Constantine says as he administers the drops on the tissue and offers the tissue to Robert while observing him a bit too closely.

Robert looks at me awkwardly as he takes the tissue and inhales 'lightly.'

We're here on a serious mission, but watching Robert coerced into inhaling the essential oil when he is skeptical of anything he ingests, puts on, or in his body is pretty comical. I'm walking away and taking my smirk with me. We'll laugh about this later. How do we engage

Constantine in a conversation conducive to our discovery without appearing too nosey?

I'm coming around the corner of one of the bookcases, having composed myself. "Robert, feeling better? How is the headache?"

"Amazingly, it seems to be going away rather quickly; now I can browse and enjoy this place better."

"This man is a Wizard when it comes to knowing just the right thing to administer to the client, aren't you, Constantine?" I say, appealing to his ego.

"I do alright; it comes with many years of studying and practice," Constantine says, putting down his glasses and puffing up like a peacock.

"So, tell me what you formulate besides what's on the shelves. I've always been curious about concoctions that may have a use for alternative means. I'm an avid Agatha Christie reader, believe it or not--and an amateur mystery writer. I've always wanted to write about an elixir that could be administered to disable an individual but would go undetected in an autopsy. Is there such a thing? Or is that just made-up nonsense from a writer's imaginings?" Robert pauses and observes. He is holding his gaze as if seeking to acquire an outer-worldly secret.

I'm mesmerized. Is it working on Constantine?

Robert continues with his quest for answers, provoking Constantine's ego. "You must forgive me if I appear too forward in my stride for knowledge. Personally, I don't think such a thing exists, or anybody is knowledgeable enough to fabricate such a phenomenal venom."

As they say in sales, the next one who speaks--loses.

"There is such a thing, I can assure you. In my travels in Asia, parts of Africa, and the remote regions of the Amazon, I've gathered secret knowledge dating hundreds of years back. Some plants, combined with particular reptile or insect venom, can deliver powerful toxicities that render an animal or human incapable of movement. Some can paralyze every muscle, including the heart, to beat enough to keep the being alive while being undetectable and unable to move at all, giving the effect of death. Only the brain may still be functional. Thoughts may still be there. This experience is so frightening to the individual that sometimes it manifests as a heart attack. Somebody could describe it as the person's body becoming its coffin.

Per your question, the exciting thing is that it travels through the body towards the heart no matter where it was adminis-tered—whether by injection or edible consumption. When an autop-sy is performed, the visible damage is around the heart's lining. Thus, the logical assumption is the person had a massive cardiac episode. Like everything in life, it has its downside."

"This is riveting, and may I use this in my writings? This informa-tion is what I wanted to know. I never encountered somebody with such an arsenal of valuable knowledge. I so appreciate this." Robert says, exuding appreciation.

With his inflated ego filling the store, he cannot stop continuing with such expository details. Somehow, this revelation feels too easy. How can this person be so intelligent and so gullible?

Constantine continues, "Like I was saying, it has a downside. The contaminants create an imperceptible odor to humans but an insult to the olfactory senses of animals. Therefore, it may not be the perfect method if you don't want the body to be found. But if you do, and you want the predators to stay away, That's the one to use." Constantine says boastfully.

Robert and I glance at each other nonchalantly. It takes a lot of re-straint not to leap and smack Constantine upside the head. He might as well have confessed to killing my friend. I must keep myself in check. We know he has the knowledge to carry on with this unspeakable crime, but we need tangible evidence to prove beyond a reasonable doubt that he committed the murder. And there is still the question, why frame me?

Robert detects my anxiety. Before I do anything that might deviate from our investigative goal, he puts his hand around my waist and escorts me closer to the door.

"Well, thank you so much for all the incredible information. You're a plethora of knowledge. I so appreciate it. How much do I owe you for the oil?"

"It's on the house. Let's call it a welcome to New Orleans gift from me," Constantine says.

"We won't take any more of your time till we meet again."

"I'll be here all night; I have inventory to log on. I'm glad I have a bed in the back, especially for nights like this. By the time I get everything on the books, I'm too tired to drive home.

"Good night, Constantine, take care!" I say, smiling and hiding my true feelings.

"I can't believe that guy. He does not show any signs of discomfort when addressing me. He is completely at ease, not nervous, egocentric, and boastful. Knowing what he has done, he doesn't show empathy at all. He can look me in the eye and not feel remorse about framing me. What is wrong with him?"

"I'm not a mental professional, but as I recall from my forensic psychology studies, this is Narcissism at its best. He believes he is so smart he is untouchable, no matter what he says or does. It is chilling to come face to face with those qualities in a person. Is a trademark of most Serial Killers." Robert says.

It was nice of him to tell us he wouldn't be home tonight. Or could it be a setup for an ambush?

Chapter 17

Night Mission

"Let's swing by my house first. I need to make sure TK and TC are okay." One can never forget the furry friends.

"Oh yes, of course, I was going to suggest that. A change of clothes can be a good thing also. This humid heat does wonders if you like the rumpled look." Robert says.

"For me, it will be a change of shoes or boots, and I must remember to take extra rubber gloves. I always have some in the truck, but we'll be on a mission."

"Speaking of mission, I did bring my field kit—which contains night vision binoculars; you can never be too prepared."

"It would be best if we go after sundown. We don't want to alert the neighbors and have somebody call him and let him know we're checking out his place. The last thing I need is an additional charge for stalking, trespassing, or worse."

"What's worse? You're already on the edge of being charged with murder." Robert says, raising an eyebrow.

"Thank you for reminding me of the imminent frame-up lurking in my life."

"I'm here to keep track of all that's going on and don't forget—to ensure you remain safe and free. Don't worry, I got you."

"But, if we get caught lurking around Constantine's property, you may be in trouble. After all, you're not acting in the capacity of FBI; you're a Joe citizen."

"There is that guy 'Joe,' again..." He says, laughing. "We're not going to be seen, we're not going to get caught, we're going to find enough evidence to put the right guy behind bars. Besides clearing you from being a suspect, we'll get justice for Antoine."

***

"Good to see you opted for the tactical boots. There are various slithering reptiles to whom we need to pay attention."

"I thought it was a good look for lurking in the dark unannounced. But tell me what other intruders I should be aware of."

"There is a nice assortment of snakes, like the Speckled King snake, which is a constrictor. It's only twelve to twenty-four inches long, so you don't need to worry about that one too much. Then there are the Cottonmouth, which is venomous, and the Copperhead, which is most active at night. Of course, since we'll be looking under wood piles and tarps, it is good to be aware and be on the lookout for these Louisiana natives. After all, we'll be lurking in their territory."

"Okay, I'm doing leather gloves, not the light forensic latex ones. There are more important things than leaving fingerprints." Robert says as he slips his gloves on.

We're rounding the corner to Constantine's house. We don't want to park too close and have a chance of being spotted. But we also don't want to park too far and be seen prowling in the darkness through the neighborhood. There is a perfect spot ahead. A large bush with a cave-like overhang is large enough to shadow and conceal the Jeep. To our advantage, I notice the glittering on the ground where the streetlights have shuttered. Tonight, darkness is our friend. The moon keeps going out of the thick cloud cover as if tonight was orchestrated. Enough light to move swiftly without falling, and when the clouds cover the moonlight, everything remains in complete obscurity and aids us in our covert mission. Of course, we're prepared for this. Besides Robert's night vision goggles, I have a small but powerful flashlight and laser. It can scatter a wide-angle beam, a slight, almost discernible halo, enough to illuminate the ground in front without being seen from afar, and the laser has the use to blind an opponent, animal or human alike, and make a getaway if need be.

"We have everything we need. Let's do this," Robert says, putting his phone on silent mode and giving me the signal to do the same.

We close the truck doors carefully, and I lock the truck with the key. It would not do to use the fob and set the alarm on. Little things like that could be detrimental to our undertaking.

Robert is in front; he looks back and signals for me to stay close behind. We see the shed at the rear of the property as soon as we clear the big bush sheltering our ride. The shed is about twenty-five to thirty yards from the back of the house. The house is dark, and there are no cars on the driveway. So far, so good. It looks like Constantine may still be at the shop.

"We're going to make a run for it till we get to the shed. There is nothing to offer cover. If a car comes around the corner, it could illuminate the area. If you see any vehicle lights coming our way or any motion detectors from the house that go on, drop to the ground. Detectors usually illuminate anywhere from seven to seventy feet. So, if we stay over that distance away from the house, we should not trigger anything if he has a system."

"Let's hope nobody comes, and nobody shines a light. I'm ready to run." I say, and instantly, we're on the move.

As if it would have it, we're halfway to our mark. Here comes a car. We drop to the ground. I hold my breath for two reasons: I don't want to make any noise and found the one puddle in the yard. Robert looks back at me, making sure I'm okay. As I look up, I see the look on his face. Yes, my face is muddy. Well, now I blend into the environment. I'll clear my eyelids, and I will continue to move forward. A little mud is not going to stop me. Now, let's get to the shed. Moving forward the last few yards and seeking refuge in the trees encircling the outbuilding gives us temporary comfort, and we can catch our breaths.

"Are you okay?" Robert asks with concern.

"I'm fine. I haven't gone for a mud mask in a while. This is good. Now, let's find something incriminating."

There are two doors to this building, one on either side. We're trying to open the door furthest away from the house. It's not locked. That's a break. We look around, and with the cover of the surrounding trees, it's safe to turn the low light so we can see what we're doing. First, we look around at the houses. The nearest one is over a hundred yards away. Most of the lights are out in the neighborhood. The ones with a blueish tinge are from televisions, so they're not looking out the windows.

"This is the airboat in question. I wonder if we'll find something, anything. Wouldn't you think Carron would have gone over it with a fine-tooth comb to eliminate any evidence?"

"Sometimes, too clean is evidence. I smell bleach; there are rags in that bucket, and they have a slight bleach odor. Why would anybody clean any vehicle with bleach? That raises a red flag. Bleach cannot eradicate traces of blood. I'm bagging one of these rags. I don't want to disturb anything and make it obvious somebody was here. Check this out—a couple of long hairs are entangled in the rags; they're coming with us. Do you know if Constantine has a lady friend who may have helped him clean up?"

"Just because it's long hair doesn't mean it has to be female."

"That's very true, and we'll take them and see who the owner of these follicles may be."

As I look at the airboat, I realize how immaculate it is. The fan in the back has dirt, debris, and mud, but the aluminum base in the front is completely spotless. I continue to check as if I keep looking for something, and it will appear. The feeling you get when you're trying to find an object and you keep looking in the same drawer over and over, thinking just once more, and the thing of your search will be right there in plain sight.

"Wait a minute, shine your flashlight over here; yours is brighter. Let me get the tweezers." I say, as my heart is pounding out of my chest.

With the rubber-tipped tweezers, I'm carefully removing a few fibers embedded in the aluminum body's front joint where the side panels join the top metal floorboard.

"Okay, let's put that in this baggy. Now, let's use some luminol and see if there are any traces of blood. Using luminol is a last resort. It deludes the markers in the blood. After its use, it is highly unlikely accurate DNA can be obtained. But at least we'll know if there was the crime scene or at least one of the transport points." Robert says with renewed optimism.

We're anxiously watching as Robert sprays his luminol on the surface. Now, turning off all flashlights, we wait in absolute darkness and see. There is no waiting as we see a blue fluorescence glow covering a portion of the front of the boat. I collapse to my knees and sob.

I'm looking down on the brittle floorboards, trying to compose myself. I see a few glowing dots and a small drip down the crevice between the boards.

"Robert, check this out and watch where you step. There might be blood spatter dripping on the floor, which may still be attainable.

"Good catch. I'll carb out the smallest sliver surrounding the drip. This old flooring is so dilapidated they'll never miss one less splinter. We may get lucky with this sample. The humidity and darkness of this shed helped retain the integrity of the droplets. I must say, I haven't seen this before, where what appears to be blood is still moist after three or four days. We must take this sample to Cecilia tonight. Let's call her and have her meet us at the lab."

I'm looking around as Robert digs out the possible evidence, giving us the clues needed to resolve this dire situation. I have a gut feeling there is something more, something here. I'm shining my light under these decrepit shelves full of webs and their dwellers, which recoil when the beam of light hits them. My light rests on a crumpled piece of paper. I instinctively take out a paper baggy envelope and carefully put it in. "You're coming with us," I say, hoping this might tie things together. We must keep hope alive.

"It's going to be a long night. First, let's make it back to the car undetected, or else all this will be for nothing."

Chapter 18

Enlightenment with Luminol

"That was a restless night. I couldn't stop seeing the glow of the luminol on the fan boat. It was disturbing. I know Antoine is dead, but to see the unquestionable appearance of blood. It made me realize he might have suffered a lot before he died." I say as I drag myself in the direction of the coffee pot.

"If this leads to a confirmation that Constantine murdered DuBois, we have to remember about the poison. According to Constantine, DuBois would have felt very little if he had administered the elixir he so proudly acclaimed. If Dubois had paralysis, he might not have the capacity to have all pain neurons firing properly, and his nerve endings may not have been able to send clear signals to the receptors in the brain. We won't know, but we must believe he may have gone in peace. And that he is at peace now."

"You're right, and we cannot sit here and torture ourselves by re-living his last minutes on this planet. We must focus on the evidence and tie the evidence to the perpetrators."

"Perpetrators? So, you're thinking there was more than one person involved in committing the crime." Robert asks.

"Or, one committed the crime and had help cleaning up the scene and maybe disposing of the body. Thus, the hair doesn't belong to Constantine. Now, we may have obtained evidence from the crime scene or at least the transport point of the decedent. Unfortunately, we gather it by trespassing, so how do we bring it to the Detective?" I say with hesitation.

"We don't. At this time, it's only circumstantial, and we don't know if the blood may be Antoine's or even human. If it's not human, we don't have a crime scene. The evidence is in good hands. I'm glad Cecilia could meet us last night and take in everything we gathered. I hope she's able to detect something substantial, something we can pursue in going after Constantine. The hairs we found could be valuable, or at least they will substantiate our findings and lead us to concrete evidence." Robert states, formulating everything in a logical sequence.

"About bringing everything to Cecilia--I forgot something."

"What is it?"

"It's a piece of crumpled paper I found while you excavated for blood. I put it in a paper envelope and stuck it in my vest. I forgot about it till you mentioned—all evidence."

"Well, let's look at it. Let's do some detecting of our own while we wait for the forensic results."

Coming back to the living room, I have to chuckle. There is Robert, with his latex gloves on and an assortment of tweezers, a magnifying glass, a strange-looking flashlight, and a digital camera at the ready. This guy is a true professional.

"Let's look and see what we can decipher," Robert says anxiously.

"Here it is, hard to make what it may be all about, but I think the spatters may be dried blood. As to who's blood, that remains a mystery."

"First, we must ensure we don't contaminate it further. The fact that you preserved it by putting it in a paper envelope is a great start." Robert says while removing the scrap of paper by the very edge with thin plastic-tipped tweezers. He is careful not to tear the already crinkled piece. Robert places it on top of the desk by the window to take advantage of the best light in the room. Of course, he turns on the light on his gigantic magnifying loupe.

"That's a bit of overkill on the super sleuth magnifying glass, right?" I ask mockingly.

"The bigger, the brighter, the better. I always say that when looking for the most elusive and minute details." Robert answers without missing a beat.

I strongly detest people looking over my shoulder when I'm working. Somehow, I'm perfectly comfortable looking over Robert's shoulder while he examines the possible evidence. I may be invading his personal space, but I have not heard any complaints. How about focusing on discovering something that may clear me of this nightmare and stop daydreaming about how cozy this situation feels now?

"Check this out," Robert says, returning me to the task.

"What is it?"

"Working from the top of the page, the first letter could either be an H or an M. Written underneath could be a 4 and clearly lbs @ $1,500. That would lead me to believe the letter may be an H for Heroin. And the $6,000 below that would be the total for the 4 lbs. something doesn't make sense. First, most drug sales are measured in kilograms.

And if he meant pounds, that stuff is way cheap, as the going price for a kilo would be around 10-15k depending on the grade."

"It sounds like this low life is a lousy businessman who may also be a weak link. That may work in our favor. We're not here to figure out somebody is getting ripped off in their illegal transactions. Let's keep up the deciphering."

"Let's continue. The next JC, obviously initials and P/U 700 pm. Now, Tommy, who the heck is Tommy?"

"I'm unfamiliar with any connection of a Tommy with Constantine Carron, but who knows? In this town, many transients are coming and going." I'm thinking of anybody I may have encountered while visiting Constantine's apothecary.

"The next part of the note doesn't seem to be related to the chicken scratches at the top. But it is much easier to make out. Meet CC house for cleanup asap."

"So, we have a note from somebody involved in dealing drugs and who does odd jobs for someone with the initials of CC. We found it in Constantine's shed, so it's safe to assume Constantine summoned this individual to come to his house and help him with some cleanup. And clean up could mean something innocent like clean up after a party or a much more ominous meaning as in clean up after mayhem and murder."

Chapter 19

Blood Findings

Robert's phone rings, making my heart jump, while he calmly answers as if he is not startled. We'll have to revisit that a little later.

"Hello Cecilia, what's the good news?"

"It depends how you look at it. The good news is that it is human blood. That could be bad news. Maybe it's good news—it doesn't belong to DuBois. The sample results came back from CODIS with stellar scores, one a career criminal who's been in and out of the grey bar hotel for most of his life. His name is Tommy Toulouse. The second marker from the hair samples belongs to another delinquent following Tommy's tracks named Jason Carron. Yes, Carron, as in Constantine's nephew. Of course, the nephew being in his uncle's shed doesn't raise any flags, but the fact they're both criminals may point in the right direction."

"That is interesting, and we'll consider where this could lead; anything else?"

"I got more for you. I took the liberty to look in the questionable subject's files. They've served time simultaneously at the same facility. On several occasions, they were busted committing crimes together. That signifies a pattern of wrongdoing. Of course, that's investigative stuff and way above my pay rate. Now that you have the names, I'm sure you, Mr. FBI man, have the resources to pull their files and do the investigating. I almost forgot that the rags from the bucket you brought me were too deteriorated to produce any detectable markers.

"Thank you, Cecilia, that's a great help. By the way, we have one other piece of the puzzle we need your assistance with."

"I'd tell you to come by and drop it off, but as you know, this is strictly off the books. So, text me where to meet, and we'll get a drink any time after 5:00 p.m. this evening."

"We'll do. At that time, we'll even buy dinner."

***

Here we are at Tony's Super Cajun Seafood, an understated establishment with an array of cuisines from fried chicken to Chinese food to authentic Cajun flavors. There is a little bit of everything, and everything is delicious. I love this place, with its comfortable booth area and smaller tables. This place lends itself exceptionally well for business meetings when one inadvertently offers to pick up the check. The prices are beyond reasonable. Robert texted Cecilia to meet us here at 6:30 p.m. As I glance at my watch, she enters with a bright smile, much more welcomed than the glaring fluorescent lights in this place. Everything must have a downside to help us appreciate the good.

"Hi Cecilia, glad to see you," Robert says, standing up and moving the chair out for her to sit.

"Cecilia, thank you for going out of your way with this. I owe you one." I say, trying to keep the quiver of emotion out of my voice.

"You owe me nothing; that's what friends are for." She says, reaching out across the table and patting my hand reassuringly. "Now, let me tell you what I got so far."

"Let's order something first. I think we can all think much clearer with food in us. I, for one, am starving." Robert states casually.

Unlike Robert, I'm not sure I can eat. My stomach is in knots. But, as I catch a whiff of the crayfish cooking, my hunger rises, and my stomach eases enough to want to order half the menu. Such a variety, I don't know what to have, or should I say, what to have first.

With the food and drinks on the table, we can relax and talk without getting kicked out for loitering.

***

When the waitress leaves the table, Robert pulls out the envelope with the note and hands it to Cecilia.

"Is this the mysterious clue that will lay all this to rest so we can go on enjoying the rest of our lives?" Cecilia asks, bringing much-needed levity to the situation.

"It would be nice if we did decipher the hieroglyphs, and now that we have names to attach to it, it makes some sense. As you can see, some stains could be blood and what appears to be a smudged fingerprint. That is where your expertise comes in."

Cecilia briefly looks at the note, carefully opening the envelope and looking inside. She's not taking it out for fear of contamination—she'll examine it at the lab under the right conditions. "I got this; I'll take it to the lab on Monday and do a work-up. If it were up to me, I would head back to the lab tonight and start on it, but I don't want to raise suspicion or let anyone know what extracurricular findings I'm working on."

"You make sense, but it will be a long weekend; waiting till Monday to hear from you and see if anything comes to the surface. Patience is not my virtue." I say with resignation.

"Cecilia is right. We need to find some concrete evidence to have something to go on. We must hope Detective LaCroix has bigger fish to fry, and he doesn't push for a quick resolution on this case. On the good side, the Detective isn't the anxious type who works overtime on any case.

"Let's hope you're right and your ability for reading people is on point. There is nothing more we can do. Let's eat, enjoy, and be present tonight; tomorrow will surely arrive with its challenges."

Chapter 20

Tears Emerge

Sitting here on my front porch admiring the glorious sunrise brings forth a cacophony of feelings. Sunrises always meant new beginnings, a chance to start again. Going out into my beloved Bayou and taking the softest and most illuminating pictures. It gave me a sense of accomplishment capturing and transforming what I saw through the camera lens and sharing the beauty with others. It was more than just a way to make a living. I was living my best life. The image of the sunrise is transposed with the image of the day when I was walking through the Bayou, and I came across Dubois' prone body—lying motionless and half covered by the marsh. A moment of a tranquil and bright daydream suddenly transforms into a grim nightmare. Shaking and unable to stand from the bench. Breathe deep, calm down. Am I helpless in this situation? How can anyone think I had anything to do with DuBois' death? He was my friend.

Tears are cascading uncontrollably down my face. I haven't allowed myself to grieve; now, I can't stop.

"Jess, what are you doing up this early?" Robert asks, surprisingly. Darn, he is coming around, and he's going to see me crying. I hate anyone to see me cry.

"Look at that sunrise; doesn't it bring tears to your eyes? It's so beautiful." I say, disguising the reason for the tears. I focus on TK and TC, who follow him everywhere within inches of his heels. They've always been a great distraction for me and helped me to change my mood instantly. Will their puppy and kitty love change my mood today? Gosh, I hope so.

"Ok, what's happening? A little moisture in the eyes at seeing the beauty from a creative such as yourself, I'll buy. But I heard the sobbing before I came out. So, let me in. What's going on?" Robert says as he sits beside me on the bench and puts his arm around me.

I might as well share; he's my friend, my confidant. It's a safe space. I'm taking a deep, cleansing breath. Breaking the silence, Robert's phone rings. He's hesitating as to whether to answer or not.

"Get it; it could be important."

"You're important. I want to hear what you have to say."

"It can wait. Now answer the darn phone; that 1950's home ringtone drives me nuts."

"Hello Cecilia, you know it's not Monday yet right?" He answers cheerfully. "Another body, the guy you said was in the shed, Tommy Toulouse. How did he die?" Robert asks and listens intently. "Ok, I'll wait for your call after you do the preliminary autopsy," Robert says, putting the phone down.

"Did I hear right; Tommy Toulouse is at the morgue? What happened? Besides the fact, he's dead."

"It appears to be an overdose, but there is bruising around his neck and upper torso. Also, ligature marks around his wrists as if he were restrained and perhaps beaten. Cecilia will proceed with the post-mortem examination and let us know what she finds."

"Well, there goes a lead that will not be reached for comment or confession. I need a coffee, and maybe I'll wake up from this nightmare."

***

"I have an idea. This whole thing started in the Bayou. We must return to the crime scene and see what we're missing. There must be an overlooked clue."

"It's been almost a week since you discovered the body, and the time of death hasn't been determined officially. Having said that... It's been long enough for any evidence left behind to be long gone."

"You're probably right, but I can't let it go. I must listen to my gut. I may be hungry for breakfast, but I'm hungrier to clear my name and find justice for DuBois."

"What are your plans?" Robert asks with a glint of excitement in his eyes.

"I'm calling Thomas Dupris. See if he can get us an airboat to the Bayou. We must come into the scene in the same manner as the perpetrators approached it in order not to miss anything."

"While you call Thomas, I'll make breakfast. That way, we'll know if it's intuition from your gut, not hunger. Always good to double-check." Robert says, smirking to the kitchen.

The phone is ringing for the fourth time. Starting to get nervous, what if something happened to Thomas? I double-checked the number. If I called the shop, maybe it would be closed on Sunday—no, I dialed Thomas' cell. I must leave a generic message for him to contact me if something happens to him. I don't want anybody with his phone to know our plan. The voice-mail message is starting.

"Hello, hello! Jessica, I'm here; I was in the shop's backroom and left the phone on the counter. I had boxes to carry. I'm sorry I'm going on. How are you doing, sweetie?"

"I'm fine. I was slightly concerned when you weren't answering, but I'm good now. Listen, I need your help. Robert and I need an airboat, and we figured you know where to get one without too many questions asked."

"Well, as they say. You came to the right guy. My cousin Jac, who we do business with regularly and takes folks out on tours, has a brigade of airboats. His business is doing quite well and growing by the minute. Sorry again, I can't help myself. Since Antoine passed, I don't have anyone to chat with daily. I find myself rambling and sometimes talking to myself." Thomas says, with his voice a bit shaky.

"I understand it's been difficult on all of us, but you saw him daily, and I know he was more than your boss. He was also a close friend. We're all hurting. That's one of the reasons I'm calling. Can you contact Jac and tell him we need to rent an airboat, cash, and no paper trail?"

"I'll do you one better; I'll go with you. I know the Bayou like the back of my hand. And as you said, Antoine was more than my boss. I want to help in any way I can."

"Is there a way you can just meet Robert and me at your cousins, and we can take it from there?"

"I know my cousin. If he's going to go off the books and assume liability, he will insist I go with you."

"Just text me the address, and we'll meet there. Are you sure you want to do this? It might be dangerous. Deep in the Bayou, we don't know what or who we will find."

"I'm sure, since Antoine's death, I felt powerless and helpless. You have allowed me to get my power back." He says with resolve.

"Would an hour or two give you enough time to meet us there?"

"No problem, I'll text you the address. I want to get there first and talk to Jac. He might need a little convincing before you two get there."

What is happening to Thomas? He is shifting into superhero mode. It might not be the wisest move to take him along into the Bayou. He's always struck me as the type who works diligently, entering data into ledgers and being thrilled when the balance sheet balances. I'm working on not judging a book by its cover, so I'll be open to his assistance. No judging.

"Breakfast is served," Robert calls from the kitchen.

"I'm not sure. I'm ready for food. Thomas insisted on coming with us on this crime scene discovery expedition. He even seemed emotionally uplifted and taking charge of talking to his cousin. He is going there first to ensure we get the airboat without paperwork, and he seems unwilling to take no for an answer. Robert, I think we've created a monster."

Chapter 21

Jac's Place

"This looks like the place; it's no wonder Jac's business is thriving. It resembles an amusement park. An area for children to play while the family waits. It is a beautiful set-up with bright, colorful shade umbrellas and picnic tables. This place is the best airboat rental I've seen." Robert observes.

"Last time I drove by an airboat rental, it looked abandoned. It had carcasses of boats tossed to the side, sharing the history of much better days and adventurous disasters in the Bayou, with parts strewn about. They were not an inviting place to walk up to and did not give the confidence that their crafts were water worthy. Now, where is our friend and liaison?"

"Here he comes. What is he wearing? The Raiders of the Lost Arc will hunt him down to get their wardrobe back. Is that netting he has on the pith helmet?" Robert asks while waving at our trusty bayou guide.

"Hi, you two. It took a little persuasion, but I handled it. I must run into the shop and get some more bug spray. In the backpack, you'll find water, a first aid kit, a machete, and other assorted necessities when trudging through the Bayou. You can never be too prepared. The boat is ready to go on the other side of the shop, see you there. Oh, one more thing: I must stop by my car to get something from the trunk." Thomas says, pointing in the general direction of the blue and white building.

"And there he goes, running to the shop. Is there anything we need to get?

How about chocolate? Anything is better with chocolate. Of course, we can only get one. In this heat, everything melts in seconds."

***

An adventure awaits in the deep of the swap. I don't want to do this, but I know I must. After all, my freedom is at stake. It's only been a week since I found Antoine. It seems like yesterday and, at the same time, an eternity. I'm glad Robert is here to share this with me and to lend a shoulder to lean on whenever I let the situation get to me.

"Where did you go?" asked Robert with a concerned voice.

"I'm right here. What do you mean? I say, trying to sound as natural as possible and not project the turmoil within.

"You had that look in your eyes, which is hard to read sometimes, but it scares me a bit."

"Scares you, nothing ever scares you. Let's get into this contraption and glide or whatever it does into the lovely marsh."

"You'd be surprised. Anything to do with your well-being and not being able to give you that terrifies me. Knowing there is evil out there and somebody trying to frame you for a murder, which is out of my control. Gives me nightmares."

"Look, Thomas is here with his supplies; now there is nothing to fear. He even brought his trusty rifle; now, what can go wrong?" I say with a chuckle, trying to defuse the seriousness of the conversation.

"We have everything we could need: plenty of water, snacks, three types of antivenom for snake bites, and did I mention a fully stocked first aid kit?" Thomas says with pride as if he has a nomination for the camp leader.

"It looks like you have enough stuff for a week or two. We're only going for a two- or three-hour tour," I say, half joking.

"Those three-hour tours can turn into a much longer unexpected stay. I'm sure you heard that before," Thomas answers, making an apparent reference to one of his favorite old shows.

"Okay, Skipper, should we get on with it?" Robert remarks, catching on to the drift of the conversation.

***

The beauty of the airboat is how it hovers over the marsh, bits of dry land, and water alike. It's exhilarating, and it almost makes you forget the task at hand. Early in the morning, it's not too hot or unbearably humid. The breeze blowing against our faces as we traverse the terrain is warm and welcome. Once in a while, we see a gator sliding from the muck and diving into the water stealthily, catching our eye and letting us know this is their home.

I point northwest to the entrance where the body was. I know it wasn't just a body, but I'm trying to keep it impersonal to concentrate without my emotions getting in the way. We must account for every detail. We must see all markings and evidence left behind. Of course, with a week having gone by, this is a challenge. There have been a couple of rainy nights, which may have deteriorated the scene. Items dropped may be in a different location. Things that may have settled on the surface may now be buried forever in the marshy soil. We must keep a sharp watch and not underestimate the value of anything linked to the crime.

Proceeding forward in the glittering water, we see droplets of dew glistening on the branches overhead, creating a canopy of greenery and dry, spiky, tangled brush. The foliage bends as if building a surreal gazebo, luring us into the Bayou. This may bring us closer to knowing what happened or eluding all discovery and leading us to a dead end.

Thomas slows down as it is hard to discern which opening will lead us to the site. Many passages lead to nowhere. We are floating over a few feet of water and hugging the shore. We're looking for the entrance which we pinpointed on the map. It looks like whoever came through here covered their path out. We know that is not possible. Logically, there is a way to the other side.

"Wait a minute, look over to the branch on the left. What's that?" I say as I spot a scrap of fabric hung up on a branch waving in the breeze.

"Let's go over there; maybe it's just a marker for navigating the waterways." Says Thomas. "Sometimes, locals mark areas to get to their hiding places, sites best for wild hog hunting or other clandestine activities.

Moving closer, we see a piece of fabric caught in dried branches. It appears stained with what could be dried blood.

"Let me pull out my evidence bag and collect this. It could be something," Robert says with hopeful anticipation.

"It could be from one of our assailants, and if we can match the blood to the samples we acquired in the shed, we may have some evidence to tie both scenes to the crime," I add.

The branches are so entangled that we shut down the propeller on the airboat. Some branches were making it through the protective cage that houses the giant fan, and flying debris was shooting in all directions. Fortunately, there is a pole to push us along this bramble entrance to the other side.

"We could go through with the propeller, but somebody could lose an eye, and we wouldn't want that," Thomas says matter-of-factly.

It is only a few feet of entanglement, and we're in the clear again. The canopy of trees is much higher now, and only the long limbs covered with moss touch the water's surface along the edges.

Instead of pushing forward on the marshy beach-like entrance, Thomas veers the airboat towards the right. We hear the sound of crushing small tree limbs and roots that poke through the surface.

"I didn't want to drive up the obvious way in, just in case there is something, tracks, or whatever may be evident to the trained eye," Thomas says humbly.

Robert replies, "That is very smart of you, great thinking. You're right; you never know what to find in this situation. I wish more people would consider preserving possible evidence like you did."

I can see Thomas's demeanor change to one of pride. And for a time, a much-needed pat on the back feeling. The poor guy has been doing so much since DuBois' demise.

We hear branches breaking as we approach, but we realize the sound is not coming from underneath the boat or the sides. It's coming from a few yards ahead.

Thomas stops the airboat, and we use the poll to get closer to the shore. We're on alert. The noise can be an animal passing by or a wild hog, which may present some issues. It may even be a rifle-toting local dweller who dislikes intruders near his property or hideout.

Chapter 22

Into the Bayou

"Don't move!" Robert whispers and signals with his left fist up while unholstering his Glock sidearm.

The signal helps as it was difficult to hear with the cacophony of bird sounds around us. There is something or someone out there. We're motionless. Suddenly, the Bayou is dead silent, as if all its creatures feel the danger ahead.

We scan the bushes, unable to sense any movement. Holding our breath and not knowing for what. Robert looks back at me. I read in his eyes to remain silent and still. I'm looking at Thomas, and he seems a little shaken but holding still in motion and determination.

A shot wooshes my head. I hit the ground instantly. Robert fires back into the bush. Can he see the assailant? We hear the muffled sound of a painful grunt.

"Are you okay?" Robert asks, looking back at us to see if we got hit.

I look over at Thomas with his face in the muck. He signals with his muddy hand and gives a thumbs up.

"We're fine," I answer, feeling the mud on my lips.

Robert says, "Stay here by the craft." Running in the direction of the fleeting shooter.

Robert disappears into the trees without giving me a chance to protest.

I am lying in the mud as if I were at a spa. The dirt contains little flies, worms, and other unidentifiable lifeforms. I'm trying to get up, but I'm stuck.

Fortunately, Thomas has freed himself from the sticky and mucky marsh, and it's cleaning his outfit with leaves.

"Thomas, can you give me a hand? Please!" I whisper, just in case the unknown assailant has come around.

"Of course, my dear, I didn't realize you were still there. This new Two Thousand Dollar, 'Sease" Endurance Jacket 3.0. will not dry clean well."

"Yes, that is the first thing that came to mind after getting shot at. How am I going to clean my outfit? And gee, I'm glad I didn't get hit, or I would have to contend with bothersome and hard-to-remove blood stains. Just get me up, will you?"

"Where is the rifle?" I ask.

"It's in the airboat. I didn't get a chance to get it before we got shot at. But I'll get it now."

"Great idea. I don't want to sit here in the muck like a sitting duck. Pardon the expression."

"Here it is," Thomas says while polishing the stock with a bit of unsoiled portion of his sleeve.

"Is it loaded, or is it a collector's item to be admired but not fired?" I speak. This situation is making me snappy. And I don't like it when

I'm snappy. It was my idea to come out here. Now, I've put two people I care about in danger.

"Let me have the rifle, please," I ask respectfully.

"You know how to handle a rifle?" Thomas says with a skeptical look in his squinting eyes.

"Yes, Thomas, I'm well trained in firearms; pictures are not the only thing I can shoot." Remember that I say smiling and winking, defusing a bit of the situation's tension.

Thomas smiles back. This brings us to the present dilemma. We haven't heard a sound other than the birds are back signing away. The sounds of scurrying animals are also audible. But where is Robert? He said to stay, but for how long? What if the shooter wasn't the only one out there? Maybe he is captured and hurt.

"I'm not going to sit here and wait any longer. You stay here with the boat just in case we need to make a quick getaway." I say to Thomas with a resolution in my voice. No questions needed.

"But wait..." I hear Thomas say. As I run in the direction, I saw Robert go and disappear into the heavy and snarled vegetation.

***

The only sound I hear is my steps crunching leaves and occasionally mushing and slurping through the muddy puddles. The birds scaw away, and suddenly, they stop. I wish I knew what it meant. Usually, it means impending peril. The sounds commence, and no sooner than I tune into the noise and try to decipher what I'm hearing, it stops again. Could there be so much danger abound? I just got my answer as I stare down a feral hog. It's about ten to twelve yards out and in my direct line of site. I raise the barrel and aim. I'm taking a deep breath and squeezing the trigger as I slowly let the air out of my lungs. I'm compensating for the adrenaline coursing through my veins and steadying myself. I only have one shot. If I miss, I'm in trouble. Wild hogs usually move in sounders, and they're not alone.

Am I ready to take a life, to save my own? As I commit, he runs towards me but veers to the left. I catch the fleeting redhead of a Broad-headed Skink lizard dashing away into the bush and the hog racing after it.

Somebody might be lunch. I'm glad it's not me. I release the trigger into a safe position and am grateful I didn't have to take a life.

I take a couple of deep breaths and am now steadying myself to continue on the path to finding Robert. How much further do I have to go to see signs of life? I did run into the bushes not long after Robert ensued pursuit, so where did he go? The birds and other wildlife are back to their orchestrated sounds. It may be safe to assume there is no imminent doom around me. Let's hope that theory holds.

Chapter 23

From Shots to Chats

I 'm hearing voices, voices in conversation. Is that Robert having a chat with someone? I'm following the conversational tone in the speech. It is Robert and another two men talking.

I can't believe my eyes. Robert is sitting on a stump with his gun holstered and holding a jar with some brownish liquid in it. One of the men is leaning against a tree along with his rifle. Never lean a rifle against a tree. The slightest movement and if it falls, somebody could get hurt. Perhaps that should not be my opening greeting.

"Hi! I hope I'm not interrupting." I say while pointing the barrel of my rifle to the ground.

"Jessica, glad you're here," Robert casually says as if seeing me at a seashore soiree. "This gentleman here is Little Tim." Pointing to the tall, broad-shouldered man leaning on the tree. "And the gentleman with the big jar of this mighty tasty beverage is Big Tim."

Big Tim is a paradox of a nickname. Big Tim is a little over five feet and weighs about one hundred and twenty pounds, soaking wet.

"Nice to meet you both," I say, raising my eyebrow in Robert's direction.

"Give the little lady a glass, will you? Where are your manners?" Says Little Tim, to Big Tim who blushes instantly.

I have not seen a man blush in a long time. Come to think of it. I don't think I've ever seen a man blush.

Before I can protest, Big Tim walks over to a wooden crate and pulls out a small glass jar. He is looking inside the container and making a face. I don't know what he is looking at. After a second or two, he shakes whatever it is to the ground. He is now whipping the glass clean with the bottom of his shirt tail and pouring some liquid into it. Great, he walks over to me with a drink in his hand. The polite thing to do is to accept it. How can I resist when he offers it to me and smiles with the widest toothless grin and a slight bow? These two are so endearing I don't know what to think. It was definitely not what I expected to find, and relieved I did. With a drink in hand, which I must keep downwind, it smells like furniture polish and turpentine. Let's see where this meeting of minds takes us.

"Robert, you want to catch me up on what these gentlemen have to say. And why did they shoot at us? Just curious."

"They did not shoot at us. They were shooting at a feral hog about to attack them. They didn't hit it; it ran away scared. And it's a good thing because, as Little Tim informed me, they didn't have a permit for hunting and wouldn't want to get in trouble with the law. His words."

"Interesting. I met their feral hog too, or maybe a close relative."

"Did you shoot it?" Big Tim asks.

"No, I couldn't shoot Pumba. Fortunately, it spotted a Red Headed Lizard and went after it."

"Pumba?" asks Little Tim. "You gave it a name."

"No, Pumba is the name of a Wild pig from a movie. The one in the movie was a Warthog, a different species and continent." I say, smiling and trying to forget that I was scared, but I will not admit it.

It's funny how a terrifying experience in one minute can bring joy and laughter a few minutes later when re-counted. Let's see what Robert has learned from these individuals, which may give us something valuable to the case. After all, that's why we're here.

I'll give Robert' the look,' which means let's get on with the pertinent intelligence without seeming pushy or rude.

***

"Guys, would you mind sharing with Jessica what you told me you saw about a week ago near where we landed the airboat?" Robert says casually.

"Sure thing. Like I was saying to Rob, may I call you Rob? I'm not one for long names." Says Little Tim, enthusiastically.

"Rob is fine...go on."

"We were out here for most of the night, setting things up for—um, you know, making our beverage, if you know what I mean. When we heard some voices coming from that area, we thought it might be the rangers, so we ducked low and hid. Next thing you know, we see two guys slogging something heavy from the front of the airboat. At one point, they were pulling, and it wasn't budging, but they pulled harder, and it gave. It appeared that whatever they were dragging off the boat got caught up on the edge of the metal surface. Anyhow, they managed to dump it by the shore. This was going on before daybreak, so it was fairly dark still, and we couldn't see what it was or who they were."

"There wasn't much light, but light enough that I saw one of the men hop on the front of the boat, pick up a rifle and scour the area. I don't know if he heard something, but he turned on a big bright flashlight and followed the beam with the rifle barrel—he was looking for something or someone. We stayed still and held our breath. We didn't know what they were doing, but we knew whatever it was, it was sketchy." Big Tim said, appearing a little shaken as if reliving the fear of the moment.

"Did you recognize their voices, or did they call each other by name?" I inquire.

Big Tim answered. "No, no, I don't recall hearing them calling each other by name. All I heard was one of them saying hurry up; we don't want to make your uncle angry, then he won't pay us."

Robert and I exchange looks. We know now Constantine is involved. At this point, all we have is hearsay. These two are not going to testify in court. They would have to divulge what they were doing in the Bayou early in the morning. They would also be relinquishing the location of their beverage-making facility. We can't convince them to testify or even go to the PD and talk to Detective LaCroix. They are forthcoming with their information, almost as if they wanted to tell someone and take the burden off their shoulders. I am surprised; they are open to sharing this information without any prodding on our part. We must seem like the trusting kind of folks. I'm pretty sure Robert "Rob" has not shared with them; he is Fed. That would put these two on the defensive and uncomfortable talking to us about what they almost saw and heard.

Robert says. "We appreciate you telling us this. After they left, did you walk up to see what they had left behind?"

You can cut the uneasiness with a knife. The two locals had been forthcoming up to this point. Now, the hesitation is apparent. Neither wants to say anything further. They're going to need a little push in the right direction.

"A friend of ours has gone missing, and we're just trying to find out what happened and if anybody saw anything that could help us," I say pleadingly.

"Well, after they left on the airboat and we could no longer hear the engine, we got up from our hiding place, knowing they weren't coming back any time soon." Little Tim shared.

Big Tim continued." We figured what they got rid of was a body. Even in the dim light, you could tell. But we didn't want to believe it. All these years trudging through the marsh, we've never come upon a human body. Mostly because the critters take care of it quickly. The gators mostly take care of anything that lands near water, and as you can see, there is a lot of that all around.

"Did you get a closer look, eventually?" Robert asks.

"We did because before they took off. The taller one got back down from the boat, and he had something with him. It was some kind of a long stick. He walked over to the bundle and placed it by it. Of course, we were curious about what it was and what it meant." Big Tim added.

"So, what was it?" I ask.

"It was the most beautiful carved walking stick I've seen. I must say, the thought of taking it did cross my mind. But we left it alone. We didn't want to get in trouble." Little Tim says.

Big Tim says. "Besides, around these parts, you got to be careful. You never take anything that belongs to the dead. It may be superstition, but I'm not willing to take a chance."

Big Tim continued." Once we saw that he was dead, we knew there was nothing we could do for him, so we walked away carefully. I got a chill running down my back. The whole thing felt wrong. There was nothing we could do. Going to the law would put us in the middle of everything. There is too much explaining to be done, which would not bring the dead guy back but get us in a heap of trouble. We talked about talking to the cops, but what if our names were thrown around in court or something? These people were killers. They may come after us to keep our mouths shut. To be honest, I'm not keen on becoming alligator bate."

Robert nods and speaks. "We understand, but sometimes you must take a chance to make things right."

Little Tim is walking around like a caged animal. His demeanor changed.

With a louder tone, he says, "I think we said enough, we don't know what happened, and we don't want to know. It's none of our business. The guy is dead, 'God Rest his Soul." But getting involved is not going to bring him back. You go on now. Best of luck finding your friend." He says, picking up his rifle, which was still leaning on the tree, and pointing with it in the direction we came from.

We know we will see them again; we must share this information with Detective LaCroix.

"Thanks for the drinks and your hospitality. You all have a good day." Robert says courteously, diffusing the elevation Little Tim's words had taken. I'm waving and smiling, hoping also to diffuse the situation. There was something said which turned the switch in the dialogue, and Little Tim, became uneasy with the conversation. After we started talking, I noticed he stopped drinking. Maybe, as he sobered up, he realized they said too much to strangers. We better pick up the pace before they change their mind about letting us go.

Chapter 24

Enough Talk, Gotta Go!

"How did it get from a simple dialogue to a dicey situation in seconds?" I say with my heart pounding as we accelerate to a run.

"It happens more often than not. You never know when, not if, things will take a turn. Let's get to the boat ASAP." Robert says, establishing the pace of firm and forward movement.

In these surroundings, you must always be aware of your footing. Your head must be on a swivel, not just looking around but up and down. Some snakes await the innocent visitor to drop by on them for a bite and dash.

Why was the distance traveled much shorter on the way there than on the way back? Perhaps because on the way there, I was listening to every sound trying to locate Robert, and now we may be running for our lives, and getting to the boat cannot happen soon enough.

"What is that?" Robert says, pointing to where the boat was beached.

I look up, and though I'm breathless, I can't help but break into laughter. Thomas has taken branches and tried to cover the front of the boat with foulage to blend into the side bushes. Is he equally disguised to blend in?

"Where is Thomas?" I ask Robert. "Do you see him anywhere?"

I hear rustling in the bushes, hoping it's Thomas.

Here he comes. I wish I could say to my surprise, but we expect this of him by now. His face is covered in mud as if on a recognizance mission. He has branches stuck on his waistband as a makeshift sniper Ghillie Suit, but instead of a sharpshooter's rifle, he is holding a gigantic hunting knife at the ready. He knows how to dress for any occasion.

"I'm glad to see you two. I was beginning to worry. I didn't know whether to go into the bush and try to find you in case you needed rescuing or stay by the boat like you ordered."

"It wasn't an order, just a logical suggestion to keep you safe. You can handle yourself and know how to remain elusive in the surroundings." Robert says without cracking up.

I know Thomas means well, but he does have a flair for the dramatic. I feel drawn to him. I hope we can make sense of all this, and once peace in my life is re-established, we can have time to grow our friendship. He is committed to helping or just should be committed. We'll see.

***

I can tell Thomas is eager to get out of here. He runs up to the boat and proceeds to de-camouflage the airboat. Of course, since he has half the bayou stuck on himself, giving him a hand makes it quite challenging.

"Thomas, let's get the branches and shrubbery off you so we don't lose an eye?" I say as I duck away.

"Oh, of course, I forgot I had all this on me, and I just want to get out of here. This outing is different than taking visitors on the occasional tour."

We're ready to head out with the boat cleared and Thomas de-branched. Now, for more fun, we must push the boat out and turn away from the beach. Robert directs me to hop up on the boat while Thomas sits at the controls and prepares to start the engine. Unfortunately, these things don't have the reverse. Robert looks around before walking into the murky waters and pushes the front of the boat, aiming it at the clear waterways. Once pointed in the right direction, we're ready to go. Robert lifts himself onto the platform of the boat. I'm looking back towards the bank and see one of our friends jutting out from the bushes and Little Tim half hiding behind a tree.

"Hit it," I command.

Thomas asks, "What's the rush? We're out of danger."

"Just go." I insist.

Robert looks back and sees them also.

"Go, go!" he yells at Thomas as Little John lifts his rifle in a shooting stance.

Thomas plunges the throttle petal to the metal without further questions. We are staying as low as possible if they decide to fire. You never know what people are thinking when fear sits in. Just as I'm thinking this, they start firing. Fortunately, they don't have a clear line to us with the rotating fan behind us. But we hear a pin or two hitting the metal of the fan cage. Thomas instantly takes evasive action and maneuvers the airboat from side to side until we gain enough distance from them and avoid the threat of getting shot.

"What was that all about?" I asked. "I thought they were okay with us."

"I guess they had second thoughts," Robert states.

"And their second thoughts were to kill us?"

"Maybe a warning not to tell anybody about them. They want to keep their secret, and apparently, they'll do whatever it takes."

"I was thinking of a way to tell Detective LaCroix about what Little and Big Tim told us, without divulging their identities and keeping them as protected informers, if you will. But now, all bets are off. They shot at us, and I don't care if their industrious beverage-making facility gets discovered and their illicit business gets shot down.

Chapter 25

No Bullet Holes?

That was more excitement than I bargained for. I'm glad to be back at Jac's airboat rental. As we get off the rig, we instantly start looking around the boat for bullet holes. It's funny how like-minds think alike. This voyage has probably bonded all three of us for life. It looks like the boat is intact, thus avoiding any uncomfortable dialogue trying to explain the outing.

"Thank you, Thomas," I say as I hug him while trying to keep some composure. After all, we put this poor guy in peril to help us.

The hug lingers a bit longer, and when he disengages, I realize by his moist eyes he, too, was trying to keep his cool.

Robert, as always, reads the room and knows when to interject and change the tone to something positive. He speaks. "How about getting something to eat while we plan the next move?

"You want me to come along?" Thomas asks.

"Well, of course, it's a requirement. We get a friend in danger; the least we can do is buy him lunch." Robert says, lightening the mood.

"Let's meet at Tony's Super Cajun Seafood," Robert suggests.

"I love that place and their Grill Shrimp Po'boy." Says Thomas.

"You got it, buddy. Shrimp Po'boys it is."

Walking to the SUV, a barrage of questions flood my mind. How are we going to present the information we gathered to Detective LaCroix? Will he believe us? I don't know why; he is not open to anything except his objective and close-minded to the truth.

"Earth to Jessica, come in, Jessica!" Robert calls out.

"Just thinking of how to present this to the detective," I speak.

"Give yourself a minute, take a breath. We're going to sit, eat, and think." Robert says while putting his arm around my shoulders.

"I am consumed with breathing outside of a prison cell. I'm in a living nightmare. We haven't heard anything from the Detective about how things are proceeding. No word on leads, nothing. That makes me nervous. I feel in his mind, this is an open and shut case."

"You know, there is no such thing as an open and shut case, even after the case is shut. There is always something more. We have great evidence; the puzzle pieces are coming together. Don't worry, or at least try not to worry too much. Let's get to Tony's and eat. We'll think better on a full stomach."

"Is that your answer for thinking, feeding the little grey cells in the brain," I speak.

"Not sure if it helps, but I know it can't hurt." He says as we hop in the SUV and take off to Tony's.

***

We managed to get ourselves presentable before walking into the restaurant. I'm glad this is a casual, welcoming place, and it doesn't have expensive upholstered seats. Nothing that cannot be wiped clean. We still have a little bit of swamp on us. I always have a change of clothes in the car to throw a clean T-shirt on. Always be prepared; that's my motto. And we will leave a large tip so they are okay with the extra cleaning at our table.

Robert walks up to the counter and orders. "We'll have 3 of your Shrimp Po'boys and fries."

"We'll bring it to you when it's ready, hon." The lady with an incredible smile at the counter says, adding a much-needed light on this day.

I am anxious, almost to the point that hunger is the last of my concerns. But eat I must to keep my strength during this ordeal. The aroma of well-seasoned cooking helps a lot. It makes me forget all the worries and concentrate on my plate.

After taking the first few mouthfuls of the savory morsels, we pause and simultaneously gather our thoughts.

Robert is the first to break the eating frenzy and brings us back to the task. Keeping me--out of the slammer.

"The way we bring the information we gathered to light is important. We can present it to Detective LaCroix but make it seem like his idea. His ego is bigger than his thought process. Unfortunately, we don't have a choice but to work with him. We give him the details, the evidence, the reasoning behind our ideas, and we drop it on his lap. Somehow, encouraging him to think, he came up with it."

"I have a question. How the heck do we do that?" I say, raising my eyebrows to the ceiling.

"The first step is figuring and deciding how to tell him how we came upon the knowledge."

"And how do we account for us going on our own to investigate?" I question.

"The fact we've gone rogue to investigate has to be turned around as the only choice he has given us. How we proceeded to gather as much evidence as we could without shining the light to higher authorities on his lack of investigative interest or ability to proceed with this case."

"Okay, we're listening."

"I can mention how, through my reach to various sources, I can bring a specialized team to investigate the case and completely remove him from the responsibility to clear it. That would not look good on his file. With his grander-than-life ego, he cannot allow that to happen."

"Isn't that coercion or manipulation?"

"Okay, so it borders on manipulation. I call it persuasion. We need to get the Detective on our side, as any escalation takes time, and we want to clear you as soon as possible. We don't want the D.A. to get involved and start charging and ordering for an arrest on the evidence they have."

"We definitely, don't want that," I say, as I start to sweat, and I know it is not due to the heat from the extra Cajun Seasoning I sprinkled on my shrimp.

Thomas has been attentively listening, eating, and not saying a word all this time. But I can see he is with us in thought.

"When do we mention we were shot at?" Thomas says a bit too loud as if coming out of a trance.

"Thomas, are you okay?" I reply.

"Yes, I'm okay. I have never been shot at before, and it just dawned on me we got shot at, and that made me angry, and I want these people to pay for it.

"I'm sorry you had to experience that. Your excellent reflexes and maneuvering of the airboat helped to keep us safe and alive. We appreciate it. You're our hero. But I understand how shocking it can be. After lunch, I suggest you go home and relax. Leave the rest up to us. You've done more than enough. Okay?" Robert says reassuringly.

Looking at Robert, I convey with a look that we said all we need to speak in front of Thomas. I'm going to the counter to order twelve Lemon Pepper chicken wings for sharing. That's an excellent way to wrap up the lunch and help Thomas forget the day's peril. Let's hope.

Chapter 26

Civil Approach

There needs to be more preparation for what we must share with the Detective. No matter what, we must tell him what we found so far. After all, the last thing I need is additional charges of withholding evidence and tampering with an ongoing investigation.

"Should we call the detective and tell him we're on our way?"

Robert says, "And allow him to scurry out of there to avoid us, no way."

"You don't think much of Detective LaCroix, do you?"

"No, I don't. This Detective is the type of person who does minimal work and expects top rewards. He doesn't want anybody to shine the light on his failures but will be first in line to collect other people's successes and call them his own. People like that in a position of authority make me ill."

"Wow, how do you really feel?" I say mockingly. Let's hope we can put some animosity aside for a civil conversation.

"But, of course, nothing but civil. I'm a professional and expressing my feelings to a confidant doesn't mean I would act in a way that would jeopardize the case. Getting you off the hook is the top priority. You can count on me."

Letting out a deep breath, hoping to center myself for what's to come. Will the Detective be receptive to what we have to share? If not, we're in trouble. Hopefully, showing up without letting him know won't ruffle his feathers.

"There is his car. So far, we're in luck," Robert says.

"How do you know that's LaCroix's car? It looks like any plain dark four-door sedan used by most detectives in this city." I question.

"The license plate. It is the same one he drove before. And usually, the detectives have a car assigned to them, and unless it gets into an accident, they're driving the same one."

"And you happened to remember the plate number?"

"Of course, it is necessary to note the smallest of details. It can come in handy in many ways. Like now, knowing he is within our grasp." Robert says, with his devastating smile.

***

Walking into the lobby of this now-familiar Station should not give me goosebumps. Why does it feel so ominous? I want to sprint out of here, go home, and put the covers over my head. I never had this feeling before. Logically, I know I can't run away from the situation. Intuition is on high alert. Will it be fight or flight?

Robert approaches the front desk and disarms the officer with his determined demeanor and sense of belonging. "Special Agent Hunt and Jessica Martin here to see Detective La Croix."

"Yes, of course, he's in his office." The officer states as if we were expected and waves us along.

"Are we welcomed guests or walking into the lion's den?" I whisper.

Robert taps lightly on the door frame as the Detective has his back to the door and is reclining back almost to a prone position. Noticing his shoulders jolt, we know we just woke him up from a nap. He's spinning around and rubbing his fingers on his temples as if getting rid of a headache. Little does he know, we're the ones who may be giving him one.

"Hello, Jessica, Agent Hunt, I was just going over some notes."

"They must be some internal notes you're referring to, as I don't see any opened files on your desk," Robert states.

"Sometimes, you just have to close your eyes and put the case in perspective." Says Detective LaCroix, getting back to his usual demeanor.

"Hopefully, you've gathered some leads about Dubois's murder. Have you interviewed any persons of interest? Somebody who may have a grudge against him. Somebody who may have owed money to him or somebody he owed money to. Anything, anything at all?

"Look, Hunt, you can't just barge in here and throw accusations and assumptions that I'm not doing my job. Or worse, inferring I don't know how to do my job. Let me remind you you're not here in an official capacity; you're just a friend of the suspect. You may think you're helping, but all you're doing is putting your nose where it doesn't belong."

"Wait a minute, what do you mean suspect?" I say, launching forward and putting both hands on his desk.

"Getting aggressive will not get you anywhere other than jail sooner than later. So, calm down and have a seat. I can't wait to hear what you two have to say." La Croix says, pointing to the two chairs.

"First of all, I am here unofficially, and that can change in a second with one phone call. I'll have so many agents breathing down your neck; you'll have no time for naps or, how did you say--contemplating cases. Let's be civil about this." Robert says, throwing me a look and diffusing a bit of my fear and anger.

A bead of perspiration makes its way down the Detective's forehead, which he wipes swiftly and assumes a semblance of control—clearing his throat as if considering what his following words will be very carefully.

"Okay, let's see what you have to say, and I'll see if it's relevant to the case."

"We know how busy you are, so to ensure we don't go over data you may have gathered already, why don't you tell us what leads you're following." Robert starts.

"Well, this is an ongoing case, and I don't feel comfortable divulging facts of our investigation with, let's say, a person of interest. I'm sure you understand." LaCroix says.

"So, you're fixated on Jessica as the subject and unwilling to look elsewhere? That narrow-mindedness doesn't solve cases; it just puts the wrong people behind bars."

"I didn't do it; he was my friend. Somebody is framing me; I don't know why. How can you sit there and be smug about it? It is my life I'm fighting for. And you're treating it like a jaywalking infraction." My blood is boiling, and I feel like pushing the stacks of neatly placed and unopened files off his desk.

"Jessica, give us a moment. Get yourself some coffee," Robert says, with a slight wink and a soft smile.

I'm stubborn, but I know when to listen. Robert has my back. Giving him time to speak to the Detective on his terms is best. He will subdue the emotionality out of the room and direct the focus to the facts. When I return to the room, I know the atmosphere will have changed, and we can present our evidence gathering in a way that can be accepted.

"Glad to see you found the coffee. The Chicory is what makes it the best, doesn't it? LaCroix says, smiling and gesturing for me to take a seat.

What did Robert do to this guy? But I want to know how to use that Superpower.

"Preliminary evidence was obtained from a shed on Constantine Carron's property. Part of the evidence was a shred of fabric, which, after testing, contained traces of human blood DNA markers. There was also a cryptic crumpled note with what could be blood spatters, and the note had what appeared to be initials and meeting times. This, in itself, is circumstantial, so we decided to visit the crime scene. We came across another piece of fabric entwined in the branches leading to the site. When this fabric was analyzed, it exhibited traces of DNA that matched a male named Jason Carron, who happens to be Constantine's nephew. It all points to Constantine Carron's involvement. Whether he did it or got these scoundrels to do it is up to the courts to prove."

"Well, well, well, looks like you're handing me the case all nicely wrapped up with a purple bow on top. Unfortunately, most of the evidence you gathered is 'Fruit of the Poison Tree.' You had no business trespassing on Carron's property. You didn't have a warrant. You might as well throw all the so-called evidence out the window. You got nothing. Just because you're a Fed doesn't mean you don't have to follow the rules. You should know better. Maybe love has blinded you and fogged your vision to see what is clear in front of everyone else's eyes. It appears that Jessica here did it, and you're trying to muddy up the waters to draw attention elsewhere."

"Wait a minute, nobody is trying to muddy anything up. We had to gather some evidence to back up our suspicions. You didn't give us anything to go on. To this day, you haven't told us what you're doing to clear Jessica. So, we had to act on our own. We had no choice." Robert says.

"We also have witnesses to the crime or at least the disposal of the body in the bayou," I add.

"Witnesses?" And how did you get these witnesses?"

"When we went back to the scene where the body was found. We took the water route to enter the bayou in the same way the perpetrators may have done it. To make a long story short, we found two individuals who, with a little prepping, divulged what they had seen."

"And these, of course, are reliable witnesses, correct?" LaCroix leans back in his chair, twirling his Montblanc pen.

"They had enough to say to substantiate that Carron's nephew was there, as one of the people who placed the body on the shore and Jessica's walking stick by it. Thus inserting Jessica into the scene." Robert explains.

With a smug look, LaCroix asks, "Can you bring me these witnesses to verify your story? All I have is hearsay—nothing to establish credibility. I'm going to have to talk to them myself. Now, where do I find them?"

"We can take you to where we met them. They have some sort of business which they would like to keep undisturbed. I'm sure they would be willing to talk to you in exchange for privacy in their endeavors. It will have to be handled delicately, to discuss without coercion." Robert says.

"So now, you're telling me how to get information from witnesses on my case. Did you identify yourself as a Fed or law enforcement in any way? Or they assumed you were frolicking through the bayou, checking out the sites, when you ran into them?"

"They shot at us when we beached the airboat, and Robert took off after them. After a bit, I grabbed the rifle and followed to make sure everything was okay. It took me a bit to find them. I was pleased; instead of bullets flying, all I could hear was voices, talking, and even a few chuckles." Adding clarity to the scenario.

"This sounds like a wild goose chase, but I will humor you, to the delight of our taxpayer's dollars. Tell me the approximate coordinates of where you found these illustrious citizens, and I'll set out with my team to find and talk to them."

"When are we doing this?" I ask.

"There is no 'We.' At this time, you're a flight risk. All the evidence I have points to one person. That person is you." LaCroix says, picking up the phone and calling an officer to come to the office.

The officer appears with a stern look on his face and deceiving kind eyes. I am confused. This guy is about to do something he doesn't want to do. What is it?

The following words drop like a hammer and my heart races.

"Read her, her rights, and place her in custody. I want this one done by the books." LaCroix says, standing up from his desk.

"Wait a minute, you can't do that." Robert objects. "You don't have any conclusive evidence. What are you doing?"

"You don't have a clue as to the evidence I have. Stand down, or you'll be joining her for obstruction of justice. As you said, you're not here on official business. Step back and let me do my job."

The officer is talking to me. I can't hear what he is saying as my heart is pounding. Something about hands behind my back: I obey, as in a dream. Then, those dreaded words manifest. You have the right to remain silent. Anything and everything you say can be held against you in a court of law. You have the right to an attorney...blah, blah, blah. Can't pass out, can't pass out now.

Chapter 27

Behind the Glass

I'm placing my hand on the glass as Robert sits on the other side of the partition and picks up the phone. He's looking at me with defeated eyes and a slight smile. He is finally getting the clue and placing his hand against the glass.

"You know it is mandatory to place the hand on the glass when visiting an inmate. It's in all the movies," I say, smiling and trying to convince him I'm not internally falling apart.

"Sorry, I don't know the rules for visiting. Usually, when I'm on this side of the glass, it's to question someone or follow up on a case. It's not chummy enough to do the hand-on-the-glass thing. It would be weird." He follows suit, making light of the situation." Robert says without missing a beat.

"So, when are you busting me out?"

"You know, they monitor these conversations," Robert chuckles. "So, for the time. We're going to do it by the book. We'll get you out the legal way. You'll be arraigned tomorrow morning, at which time the court will set bail. I'll take care of the bail, and you'll be out by the afternoon."

"Should I be getting a lawyer?"

"I already reached out to a long-time friend who's one of Louisiana's best Criminal Defense Attorneys. His office is in Baton Rouge. His name is Clark Roman. He already set in motion a ROR, released on personal recognizance or signature release."

"I feel better knowing there is somebody we can trust. It's all happening so quickly." I speak.

"Much too quickly, according to Clark. Per Louisiana law, the District Attorney has more than one hundred days to press charges in a homicide case. This overzealous overnight situation is highly unusual." Robert explains.

"I'll take overzealous as long as I get out of here as soon as possible. Once I'm out, we'll get to the bottom of this.

I can't believe I'll be spending the night in jail. How are TK and TC going to cope? They've never been left alone."

"They won't be alone; I'll ensure they're taken care of."

"No offense, but you're not their mommy. They have a routine and a space on the bed. If things are not according to their expectations, they won't get any sleep."

"In that case, forget about the legalities of getting you out of jail and brief me on the important details of what I need to do to make sure your cat and dog get their good night's rest." He thoughtfully says as he pulls out his notebook and prepares to take notes.

"I brought you a change of clothes to wear in court. They will bring them to you before they transport you to appear for the arraignment."

"Well, thank you. I was not thinking about that at all. I guess the prison t-shirt and workout pants give the presumption of guilt. I appreciate you being here for me through this ordeal." I say, blinking my eyes one too many times to keep the tears from flowing.

Having red eyes and seeming vulnerable is not a good look if you want to pretend you can hold your own. I know this is temporary, but every minute is an eternity. I've never been so frightened. If things go sideways, this could be my life. No, I won't go there; negative thoughts bring negative results. I am staying positive no matter what.

"I'll see you in the morning," Robert says brightly and hopefully.

I smile back and swallow the lump in my throat. I can hang in there for a few more hours. I'm going to go back to my cell, those are words I never thought I think—and I'm going to practice sleeping with one eye open.

Reality sets in as Robert hangs up the phone, stands up, and, with a quick wave, walks away. My shoulders droop, and I choke down tears. I never thought, in a million years, I would have this experience. They say, 'everything happens for a reason,' but I'm stuck on what the heck the reason could be for this. I'm Taking a deep breath, straightening myself up, wiping my face with the sleeve on my lovely beige scrubs, ready to join the line going back to confinement.

***

There is a hum of voices throughout the court. I see Robert sitting close to a distinguished, salt-and-pepper-haired gentleman. He must be Clark Roman, Attorney at Law. If he isn't, he definitely could play one on TV. We are directed to go single file and stand up against one wall, with the Sheriff's deputies on either of the six of us, who are being arraigned this morning. Once again, we're guided to sit on the bench. As we file in, the handcuffs are removed. I thank the deputy with a nod. Nobody is talking, as we were told not to speak, especially to each other while in court. This situation is intimidating, not knowing what to expect. This situation happened much too quickly. I didn't have a chance to be briefed by my attorney. I thought that was weird. Mr. Roman had attempted to visit me at the jail. I got a note covertly passed by a deputy as I entered the transport. It said my attorney had been there but was made to wait until it was time to go to court. I wondered why she gave me the note. I've never given up hope there are good people in all places. People who try to do the right thing when they see injustice happening. Why was he kept waiting, and I wasn't allowed counsel? Oh well, I'm here. I intend to do what my attorney guides me to say and do. Speak only when directly addressed to do so—and not panic. I should have led with the No Panic part.

"All Rise." It's said loud and clear by the Bailiff. The Orleans Parish Criminal District Court is now in session, The Honorable Judge Joseph Jacobs presiding. Be seated."

As the attendants sit in unison, the air in the room seems sucked out. This just became real. Too real. The anticipation is tangible. I want to get this over with, but at the same time, I want to prolong the time in case this is my last chance at freedom if you can call it that. This experience is surreal. I'm listening to fellow arrestees go in front of the Judge, and I'm trying to determine the Judge's disposition in the cases. Not knowing the details of the individual charges makes it hard to decide whether he is a fair or vindictive judge. Did I hear my name?

"Jessica Martin, come up to the podium." The Bailiff announces with a tone.

I was so in my head that I didn't hear it the first time. Great, I'm already messing up. As I move forward, I'm relieved to see the attorney moving toward the podium. I won't face this alone.

"Jessica, I'm here to represent you. You won't need to say anything unless the Judge asks you direct questions. I'll take it from here." Clark Roman says and gives me the confidence to take another breath.

The Judge takes a moment to look through the file on the bench. He is shuffling pages back and forth. He's nodding his head from side to side and raising an eyebrow. What is the meaning of all that? He motions the Clerk over and whispers something to her while covering the microscope with his hand. The Clerk shrugs her shoulders lightly and goes back to her desk.

"We have People vs. Ms. Jessica Martin's file—case in front of me." says the Judge, with a questioning tone.

"Your Honor, I'm Clark Roman, stating for the record, I will be representing Ms. Martin in this case."

"Good to have you in my court again, Clark," States the Judge with familiarity. "I must admit, this case has me questioning why Ms. Martin is in front of me in the first place. I didn't have a chance to review the case before sitting at my bench; honestly, there is not much to review. Let's proceed and work with what we have. It states the charges are Murder in the first degree. Yet, there is not a shred of conclusive evidence presented. I feel this case was brought to me prematurely and without merit. To expedite the arraignment and these procedures, let me ask you, Ms. Martin. How do you plead?"

"Not guilty, your Honor," I say with absolute resolution.

"Your Honor, I would like to present that the defendant be ROR--Released on her recognizance. She has no prior offenses and has never been in trouble with the law. She's a homeowner with permanent residence in New Orleans and doesn't pose a flight risk." Clark states to the court.

"I agree. I state that Ms. Jessica Martin be ROR."

"I object, she's a murderer." Detective LaCroix yells, shuttering the decorum.

"Silence, you will not shout in my court." The stern side of the Judge is apparent.

"Your honor, she killed a man. She needs to be in jail where she belongs." LaCroix continues.

"One more outburst from you, and you'll be in contempt. Detective LaCroix. Yes, I know who you are, and I don't like your presumption of guilt. Let me warn you since you decided to make a mockery of my court. Next time you present a case for charges to the D.A., you better have a foundation based on conclusive evidence. I don't respond well when the court's time is abused. Am I clear?" The Judge states a rhetorical question.

"Yes, your Honor," LaCroix answers, sending a chilling look in my direction. The threatening look doesn't go unnoticed by the Judge.

"This is an unusual circumstance. Therefore, I rule that Ms. Martin be released forthwith from this court. She will not return to jail; all necessary paperwork will be directed to the court and her attorney. I see no reason for Ms. Martin to spend one minute without her freedom. Ms. Martin, you are free to go."

I'm looking at the Judge with tears in my eyes and managing to say, "Thank you, your Honor."

Chapter 28

Jail Bird

"I'm out. I can't believe it. Is this real?" I say as I let the Sun kiss my face. "I can't wait to shower and wash the jail smell off me."

"How about getting some real food in you?" Robert asks.

"I just want to go home, be with my furry babies, take a shower, and then eat. You can order delivery while I clean up. I want to enjoy my freedom and sleep in my bed tonight. I can appreciate the little things more now that that nightmare is over."

"I hate to be the bearer of bad news, but the nightmare is not over. You're still a suspect in LaCroix crosshairs. He is like a dog with a bone. He's not giving up. We must find out why he is determined to put you away. There is a big picture here we're not seeing. At least not yet, but if we put on our thinking caps and start looking for underlying motives, we will find it." Robert says as he taps my hand reassuringly.

"Go there! They have my favorite fried chicken, and they have a drive-through." I say, pointing and trying not to reach for the wheel. I'm ravenous all of a sudden.

***

"If there was no merit to the case, no conclusive evidence to substantiate an arrest per the judge, how did it get past the D.A.?" I say as I bust out of my room, still towel-drying my hair.

"I have the feeling Detective LaCroix and our newly appointed D.A. may know each other in a way more than just working in the law system together. There is no way an impartial D.A., who doesn't have something to gain, would have presented something so feeble in front of a judge. The reputation of the D.A. follows them from case to case. Unless there is coercion or some cover-up, maybe she owes LaCroix a favor. I'm thinking aloud, but something doesn't add up." Robert says.

"Who is the D.A., in this case? I saw a young lady on the prosecution side of the court. I noticed she left the court with a phone to her ear as soon as we were seated when the Judge came in. Was that the D.A.?

"I'll give Clark a call. He will have the paperwork from the court. That's why he didn't walk out with us. I think he wanted to have a chat with the Judge. It seems they go back a bit, and that will surely help. I hope he can do it without muddying up the waters." Robert says as he reaches for the phone.

"Clark, this is Robert. Give me a callback. We need to strategize about the case and give you some insight we've been discussing. Maybe we can meet for lunch tomorrow—text me what time and where—you're a man of good taste. You pick the place—I pick the tab." Robert hangs up as he walks to the kitchen, closely followed by TK.

Robert comes out of the kitchen, followed by TK, the little dog practicing pursue mode. She doesn't give up. He is bringing a bottle of wine and two glasses. It must be a relaxing time.

Robert's cell dings. He picks it up and smiles. "Clark texted he wants to meet at Antoine's Restaurant tomorrow at twelve-thirty. That man has excellent taste. Antoine's Restaurant was started by an 18-year-old named Antoine Alciatore in 1840. The food and the ambiance are the best."

"Would you mind if I meet you there a bit later? It will give you time to catch up. I need to go for a short drive and clear my head. I know I'm out and wasn't in for that long. But I still feel confined somehow."

"I get it. I'm smothering you already," Robert says, smirking.

"No, definitely not. I'll never be able to thank you enough. I need time with my thoughts, and driving has always been my go-to thing. I'll leave here around eleven thirty and meet you there no later than one.

Chapter 29

What's your Emergency?

I have a good feeling about this. When things seem like they can't get any worse, it is when things usually start to upright themselves. Just driving makes me feel like myself and in control. I take a side road to be alone, and somebody else has the same idea. This road doesn't go very far, and it's not paved for speed. I'll pull as much as possible to the side and let him pass. He seems to be in a hurry. 'Okay buddy, go ahead and pass,' I say as if he could hear me as I motion him—to go around. He is picking up speed, so I guess he finally got the picture. I do not want to race with his old beat-up rust and white van. Now, he's slowing down. Really? I'm not in the mood for games. Wow, what is wrong with him? He just about hit my bumper. I'm calling 911. Maybe things can get worse.

"911, what is your emergency?"

"I'm on Recovery Dr. going north past the..."

"Are you still there? You cut off, repeat your location. Are you there?"

***

What just happened? Okay, remain calm and check out the surroundings. First, am I badly hurt besides the gush on my forehead? I'm breathing, and the only thing that hurts is my head. That's not too bad. Find the phone and continue the conversation with the lovely 911 lady. Where is my phone? Great! It went out the window. The seat belt is hurting; it is not designed to keep a body comfortable when the vehicle is on its side. I need to get out. I'll climb out the window without unnecessary kicking and flailing. Humor is better than panic in these situations. I'm hanging on the door and twisting my body towards the window before unfastening the seat belt. Okay, Jessica, you got this. I lift myself out the window with one swift thrust, pushing off the middle council. Great! Landing face first in the tall, wet grass. My beloved SUV slides down towards the marsh and temporarily is held in place by a tree trunk protruding from its watery grave.

I must go up the slippery and marshy embankment to the road. It looks like it got pushed off the road between small trees and bushes. I'll traverse the hill towards them and make my way up with their help. Bloody hands from grabbing the branches and climbing now match the bloody forehead. I must be a site. Definitely not suited to appear at Antoine's Restaurant. First things first, only a few more feet to the road, and I should be able to flag a ride. Suppose they don't mind picking up somebody looking like a bloody Zombie. I'm pretty close to civilization, I can walk to the Truck repair on Chef Menteur

Hwy. They'll hopefully recognize me since I brought my SUV there for service and not shoot on sight.

The sweat mixed with blood is blinding me. I must wipe this off my face. My cotton pashmina needs to be more than a fashion statement. No amount of soda water will get these stains out. Oh well.

That can't be. The van that ran me off the road is sitting there. Why would he be sitting there? I got my answer from the smoke flowing out of the windows. So, he runs me off the road, sits there, and rejoices by smoking the side salad--really?

Now what? I can't go back to the marsh. I could go back down a bit off the road temporarily and hang on the branches till he drives away. Too late, he saw me. I'll go on the opposite side of the road and run as fast as I can. How quickly can he go on reverse? This road is narrow, so turning around will be challenging, especially if he is as stone as the smoke bellowing from the van would suggest. I can't believe it; he is keeping up and about to overtake me. How can that be?

He is running towards me, and I have nowhere to go. Fight with might. That's all I can do. Wait a minute, I know you, you're Little Tim. Oh no, not a Taser.

***

"It's One forty-five; Jessica should be here by now. She's always on time, and if something came up. She would have called."

"Call her, see where she is. Maybe she had car trouble," Clark says.

"It just rings and goes to voicemail. Something is wrong," Robert states. "I have a friend who works for Emergency Response. I'll call her and see if they received any 911 calls which seem suspicious. Hi Angela. This is Robert Hunt. I need your help."

Angela asks. "Is this in an official capacity or personal?"

"Personal, but it may be an emergency. I need to locate a friend of mine. She was going to go for a drive and then meet her attorney and me for lunch. She's late, and she is never late. Her phone goes to voicemail. I need to know if any calls that went unanswered or disconnected came in between eleven thirty and one forty-five this afternoon. Or even dispatch to a hospital?

"Actually, the gal beside me had a strange call from someone driving, and the line went dead. I'll patch you to her."

"Thank you, Angela, I'll be in touch."

"Robert, this is Patty. Angela says you are trying to find a friend who may be in trouble. I did get a call around noon, which was disconnected. We've dispatched a unit since the person was able to give us an approximate location. She said she was on Recovery Dr. going north, past—that's when I lost her. There was a loud noise, like metal against metal. I did get confirmation a few minutes ago that the police, along with the fire department, were on site. A vehicle, some SUV, apparently went off the road and is hanging precariously above a waterway."

"Did they find anybody in the vehicle? My friend's name is Jessica Martin. Please pass the information to the units on site. That way, they can verify that it is her vehicle. I'll be on my way." Robert says anxiously.

***

"I'm glad you're riding with me, Clark. I've seen way too many scenes like this in my career. This is different, this is Jessica."

"Don't worry, Robert, we'll find her. I'm sure she's all right. After all, she's not in the vehicle. She most likely made her way up the road unharmed and was picked up by a good Samaritan."

"Thanks for the positive outlook. I definitely can use it," Robert says. "Let's go ask some questions and find our girl."

***

"Every emergency vehicle in town has been summoned to this location. With that many eyeballs, they have to have something. Let's go see what they have."

"Who's the incident commander on the scene? I'm special Agent Hunt. And this is my friend Clark..."

"I know Clark. I testified on one of his cases a while back. How are you doing, Clark? It's been a bit. You got to stop by more often. How can I help you, folks?"

"Johnny, nice to see you. Thanks again for your testimony. It made a real difference." Clark says, being cordial.

Robert's patience is dissolving quickly. "This is all nice, but we're wasting time. Reminder: Jessica is missing, and we're here to find her and ensure she's safe. Again, can you point us to the person in charge?"

"We're walking in the right direction. No need to get huffy. This is not the big city. We do things on our own time." Says the deputy.

"Wait a minute, what is this? It looks like a piece of bumper lying on the road right before the skid marks begin. Has this area been processed?"

"Heck no, we just got here."

"I suggest you put a marker on it; nobody touches it unless they're part of the forensic team. This area needs to be cordoned off. This is no ordinary accident; this is a crime scene."

Chapter 30

What a Ride

Where am I? And what is that awful smell? It's like something died in here. I have to get out. Why is Little Tim doing this to me? Okay, first things first, get rid of the blindfold. And the dirty rag tied over my mouth. I want to catch my breath, but with every breath, I'm gagging with the fowl pungent odor of this van. My body still feels numb, but I must fight it. Rubbing my head against the side of some wooden object seems to help. Here it comes. I think I'm going to be ill. The thing I was rubbing against was a dead wild pig's task. Looks like you're going to help me get the rag out of my mouth. I'll shower for a month later. It's working, it's coming loose. Now, there is a find—a knife laying in plain sight.

I can wiggle myself to it quietly, I hope. So glad to see there is a partition between the back and the driver's compartment. Did they do that to keep the aroma of their fresh kill out of their nostrils? I'm not going to speculate. I must cut myself loose and prepare to escape when he tries to get me out—maneuvering like a crab, grabbing the knife, and figuring out how to cut the ropes without attaining severe injury. Ouch, easier said than done. My fingers still tingle from the taser, and now I'm cut. Let's try again. Hands are free, now the feet. I got it. The van is stopping. My heart is pounding. I'm ready. I must be ready.

The door opens, and I launch like a wild animal, knife at the ready. I strike the man on the left shoulder, and as he clutches his shoulder with the right hand, I hit again on his mid-side. He goes down. I don't want to kill anyone. I feel like I know him, but I must get away. I'm looking around to see if anybody else is coming. I hear nothing other than the struggling breath from Little Tim. By the small amount of blood pooling, I don't think he sustained any lethal injuries. Maybe I can get some answers.

"Who sent you for me? I can finish the job. You didn't do this on your own. Now tell me, who asks you to run me off the road and kidnap me? Where were you taking me?" I say, stepping on his shoulder against everything I hold dear to help him cooperate.

He screams, saying, "I can't say, he'll kill me. He has eyes everywhere."

"What makes you think I won't?"

"He has Big Tim. He said he would kill him if I didn't bring you to him. He would burn down our place in the Bayou with Tim in it." Little Tim says as he's starting to fade.

"One last time, who asked you to do this?" As I crouch down to hear him.

Exhaling, he whispers. "He is the la..."

The birds are silent, and the breeze seems to have stopped. In the dead silence, I hear branches breaking, and muffled voices. I have to get out of here. I'll take the van, thank you.

***

"Look, over there, there is a reflection coming from where the car is. Let's check it out." Robert says.

Clark replies. "You check it out. With these shoes, I'm liable to slide into an alligator's mouth at the bottom of the slope."

"That's right, you do all your fancy footwork in court. I'll head down and see what it is."

"Hey Clark, found Jessica's phone. She'll be happy to know that when we find her, but now that we know she doesn't have her phone, it will be more difficult to trace her."

"What next?" Clark questions, raising an eyebrow.

"I'll take the phone to the FBI office on Simon Blvd. and see if they can clear up the sound and amplify it, if possible. If the line remained open, we could hear something or someone who may lead somewhere."

"Is not much, but it's something," Clark adds.

"Not much we can do here. The forensic team will gather all the evidence, including the bumper's piece. It's time I contact my colleagues in NOLA. It just became a missing persons case."

"In the spirit of collaboration, will you tell the lead detective that you'll be taking the phone for examination to the Feds?"

"You're right, everything out in the open, is the best way to go. Here comes your buddy Deputy Johnny, running at us. I wonder what's so urgent."

Between breaths, Johnny manages to speak. "A van just crossed our containment line at the end of the street. It zig-zagged through the barrier, and it's making its way towards us. See it there? A car was close behind, but they pulled a U-ie and burned rubber away from the deputies. Hold your cover behind these vehicles until we know who's driving. It will be treated as a Felony stop if they decide to stop."

"Okay, Okay, we'll follow your lead. We'll stay put."

"Can you see who the driver is?" Questions Clark.

"I have a pair of binoculars in the car."

***

Robert yells, "It's Jessica! Take these."

"Are you sure?" Clark asks without expecting an answer as he watches his friend run through the labyrinth of police vehicles shouting, 'Stand Down, Stand Down' It's Jessica.

I did not expect this reception, but I'll take it. And there is the most welcome site, Robert running at me in slow motion, not really, but if this were a movie, it would be cool. I've never been more relieved I'm alive.

"Jessica, are you okay?" Robert asks as he squeezes me in a tight embrace.

"I'm okay, but I'm having trouble breathing."

"We'll call a medic over to check you out."

"No need, as long as you stop squeezing. I'll be fine." I say, smiling.

He's finally releasing me and smiling. "I see you're back to your old self. Let's get you checked out anyway. You have a laceration on your head, have to make sure you don't have a concussion. Also, they'll have to preserve your clothes for any evidence leading to the perpetrators. Plus, the authorities will have to debrief you as to what happened and if you can give them an idea of who is involved.

"I just want to go home, take a long shower, and even a longer nap. But I know there is a procedure to follow. So, no lunch at Antoine's?"

I'll embarrass myself by breaking down and crying if I don't joke. Joking is all I got.

"Oh my, there is my Jeep, ready to go on the flatbed. Where are they taking it?" I ask as I feel melancholy. I love my wheels.

"It will be taken into evidence, as you know, somebody pushed off the road. It was no accident since a kidnapping took place." Robert says.

"Yes, of course, I understand. My head is still swirling from today's events. The bump on my head is starting to throb. The adrenaline is wearing off."

"We are going to the hospital--I'll tell the Sheriff; he can meet us there. Unless you want to ride in the ambulance."

"No ambulance for me, too much like the back of the van. By the way, I know who the kidnapper was."

"Who was he?"

"Your drinking buddy from the Bayou, Little Tim." I welcome sitting in the car, knowing I'm safe for now.

"Hi Jessica, we have to stop having these short meetings," Clark says, reaching out and tapping my shoulder from the back seat.

"Yes, like a nice lunch at Antoine's and no case to defend," I say. "I'll take a raincheck for that."

"You got it. First, let's find out who's behind this. The running you off the road and kidnapping are not random." Clark says.

Robert adds. "The fact that Little Tim is the perpetrator right after we informed Detective LaCroix, Little Tim, and Big Tim were witnesses to the disposal of the body has me thinking. What ties these two with the Detective? Did he know them before, or did he somehow enlist them to do his bidding?"

"Do you think LaCroix's lack of perseverance is because he's covering up for somebody or in some way directly involved in DuBois's murder?" I question. I'm getting a headache, not sure if it's from the bump on my head, or just thinking too hard. This situation is getting more entangled by the minute. And to think about it, we still don't know who could have entered my place and stolen my walking stick. All I know is they were stealthy, as TK never barked. Of course, she was in my room, in my bed, and under the covers. She's lucky she's so cute because she's not much of a watchdog.

Chapter 31

Hospital Safety

"I didn't expect to have an escort to the hospital," I say.

"As you know, keeping the chain of custody and evidence is all. Right now, you and your clothes are part of that evidence." Robert reminds me without sounding condescending.

"I remember it all too well. Everything needs coding, noting, categorizing, and booking. This situation puts me back to the attack in Los Angeles, back at the hospital. I had to submit to the same scrutiny, interrogation, and humiliation. It's as if history is repeating itself. No matter where I go, violence follows me." I say, feeling defeated.

When the car stops, a female deputy with kind eyes and a warm smile appears at the door. She escorts me to the ER entrance, and Clark and Robert follow close behind.

A nurse meets us at the entrance and asks us to follow her to a room. This is an actual room, not one separated by a curtain. I'm relieved about that. It should keep the humiliation to a manageable degree. Even though I am the victim in this scenario, why do I feel like a felon? Maybe it's the deputy getting the evidence packaging ready to bag my clothes. It could also be the two deputies guarding the door. I feel cold and alone, though the temperature is in the mid-eighties, and Robert and Clark are just a few feet away, on the other side of the door.

The nurse enters and hands me a gown. She tells me to disrobe and pass all the clothing to the deputy. Whose gloved hands carefully handle the garments and place them individually in the paper bags. I'm following directions up to a point. I hand my blouse to the deputy, along with my slacks. My socks and shoes are also carefully placed in their bags. I can see how the soles of shoes would be of importance. I keep my undergarments, after all; at no time were they exposed to the elements or anybody's grabby hands.

"Those too." The nurse points to the undergarments with unneeded authority.

"I think not," I respond with equal resolve. "It's not that kind of case. I never lost my shirt or pants. Therefore, there is no need to test anything else for evidence. You can go now and tell the doctor I'm ready."

Before she gets a chance to argue, the deputy reinforces my wishes. "Nurse, you can get the doctor now, " the deputy says while moving to the corner table to tag, label, and record the evidence.

"Thank you, Deputy...?" I say as I try to read her name tag.

"My name is Margarita Sanchez. Here to serve and protect against Nurse Ratched." She chuckles.

"Will you be staying while the doctor checks me out?" I question.

"I will be staying as long as it takes me to write the police ID number, the date, time, and description of the item. I want to make sure all the pertinent information is correct."

"So, you won't be questioning me about the events that led me to be here today?"

"That's above my pay rate. That's detective work, maybe someday. I believe Detective LaCroix is on his way." She states, rolling her eyes.

"You know the detective?" The roll of the eyes piqued my curiosity.

"I know of him. I'd rather not say anything negative." She says, averting her eyes and getting back to her tagging.

"So, there are negative things to say that you would much rather not say. Come on, it's just us gals here. Let me in on the gossip." I say, trying not to seem too intrusive but hoping to gather whatever dirt she may have on our beloved Detective.

"Miss Jessica Martin, I'm Doctor Tran, here to care for you." He says with a caring smile.

Just when I was going to get some juicy stuff on our Detective, oh well, it will have to wait.

"I'm ready to be taken care of and released as soon as possible," I say.

"Ok, let's take a look." Doctor Tran says while shining a much too bright tiny flashlight into my eyeballs. "It appears you do have a concussion; I would like to run some tests to ensure there is no internal bleeding or other complications. With head injuries, you can never be too careful. I'll have the nurse come in to clean the wound. I don't think you'll need stitches. We'll know for sure once it's cleaned. The cuts on your hands are superficial. A good cleaning, disinfecting, and a tetanus shot will do the trick."

"Thank you, doctor. I really feel fine. I want to go home as soon as possible." I say as I stand up from the edge of the bed, and the room starts to spin.

"Lay back down, relax. A little dizziness is not unusual in these cases. You've gone through a lot. I'm ordering an MRI just to be safe."

I almost had him convinced. The clutching of his lab coat to keep me from falling didn't help. Darn, now, I have to stay longer.

"Hello, Miss Martin, how are we doing? I'm here to take good care of you. Says a new nurse with the most delightful Jamaican accent.

I must have dozed off since I was woken up. Or did I pass out? I hope it wasn't the latter.

"Oh, Hi! Yes, I'm ready for the cleanup and to get out of here. I don't like hospitals.

"Honey, I'll let you in on a little secret. No one does." She laughs. "I'll have you fixed up in no time.

Hospitals are busy places. Whenever you can get some shut-eye, somebody checks your vitals or takes you somewhere. Now that the MRI is done, I have to wait for the results; maybe I can get some rest. The MRI with all the metal-on-metal clinging noise gave me a headache on top of the headache I already had. It was like being inside a giant speaker at a techno concert.

"Per doctor's orders, we will administer some saline solution. It will help with your hydration. Might as well hydrate while you wait." Nurse Wonderful says, laughing at her unintentional rhyme.

"Whatever the doctor says, I just want to sleep. I'm exhausted."

"I'm going to close the shades, shut the door, and let you rest. We got swamped, so the doctor will be a minute before he returns with the results. You rest now, Okay?" She whispers and lightly tiptoes out of the room.

***

I wonder how long I slept; I feel much better. The room is shaded enough to allow for an easy entry into wakefulness. Stretching feels good, except for the pull on my left arm. The fluid line is stuck on something.

"Who the heck are you? Get out of my room. Nurse! Nurse!" I yell. Where is the button? As I scramble through the sheets to grab it.

"Take it easy, is me, Detective LaCroix." He says with a slight chuckle to his voice.

"What are you doing here? Why are you standing in the dark? What are you doing with the fluids?" Get out!

"Come down, Jessica, you're acting delusional. I just came in to ask you some questions about the alleged kidnapping." He says calmly.

"What were you doing or trying to do to my fluid line? I felt the tug. I didn't imagine that." I ask as my heart races, wondering how long it takes to get a nurse here.

Still standing in semi-silhouette and with his right hand in his pocket, he says mockingly. "You need to stop reading crime novels; not everybody is out to get you, or maybe they are. Either way, you must answer my questions."

"Where is Robert and Clark?" I shout.

"That sounds like a law firm, and believe me, you're going to need all the legal help you can get to get you off for murder." He continues condescendingly.

Robert enters, followed by Clark, hitting the light switch and hopefully bringing some light into this scenario. "Jessica, are you ok?" And why are you here? Robert says, directing his eyes towards the Detective as Clark moves to the blinds and opens them.

"I'm here to ask questions, which is my job, especially when an allegation of a kidnapping is thrown in the mix of a murder investigation. Why would you be surprised that I'm here?"

"Jessica is currently under a doctor's care. We'll come down to the station when she's well enough. Until then, you're not to go near her. Or you can be facing harassment charges." Robert says, gesturing towards the door.

"Wait! He has something in his pocket. He was pulling on the line. He was going to put something in it." I shout in desperation.

"Jessica, you have a vivid imagination. Maybe you should be a writer instead of a photographer. Let me know when you can come down to the station. Make it sooner than later." LaCroix says, pushing his way out the door.

"Why didn't you stop and frisk him? I know he had something in his pocket. I think he was trying to kill me."

"Now, Jessica, that's a grave allegation."

"Yes, it is, and I'm dead serious about it. I felt the tug on the line. If I didn't wake up in time, I may have never woken up again. That guy is up to something. I can feel it in my bones. I thought you two were outside the door." I say, trying not to be too emotional or needy.

"The head nurse told us to go and sit in the waiting room, that you were resting, and she would let us know when you were ready for visitors," Robert says.

"When did she tell you this?" I ask.

"About 10 minutes before us hearing you shouting," Clark says, looking at his watch.

"So, just enough time for the Detective to sneak in here. Interesting. I have a feeling LaCroix is behind that message." Hopefully, I'm not sounding too paranoid.

Robert exits the room, saying, "I'll ask her if the detective said anything to her."

The good doctor enters the room with a warm and apologetic smile as Robert exits the room. "I'm sorry it took so long to get back with the results. I have good news. There are no signs of abnormalities, bleeding, or contusions. You're clear to go. I'll have the nurse prepare you for discharge. You take care."

"Thank you, Dr. Tran. I can use the good news, and no offense, I can't wait to get out here," I say, already swinging my legs over the bed, realizing I can't go far on two counts. One, I'm still attached to the drip; two, all my clothes are in evidence, and all I have is this lovely gown.

"Are you ready to go? let me get you unplugged." Says Jasmine, with her infectious smile. "More than ready, except that I have nothing to wear. Could you get me some scrubs or something?" I plead.

"No need. The cavalry is here," Renee says. "Robert called and told me what happened and that you were getting discharged. I swung by your place and picked up some clothes and shoes. And left a crockpot with hearty Jambalaya waiting for you."

"Thank you, Renee. You don't even know how grateful I am. You guys think of everything."

Renee says. "That's what friends are for. We got your back. Get dressed, and let's get you out of here."

Robert comes back in as I sit on the corner chair, looking out the window and feeling the warmth of the Sun coming through the glass. I can't wait to be outside, away from the distinctive hospital smell. The look on his face concerns me. It may be anger, frustration, or something else.

"Robert, what's wrong," I ask.

"I went to ask the head nurse if Detective LaCroix spoke to her. After she told us to sit in the waiting room and not disturb you, she told Jasmine, your nurse, she had a family emergency and had to go. She still had a few hours on her shift, and they had to scramble to get somebody to sub for her."

"So, we have no idea if LaCroix was behind you two not being around the door," I ask.

"Actually, we do. Jasmine, who's most observant, saw the Detective speak to the nurse, but she couldn't hear the conversation. But the body language told her it wasn't a friendly exchange. Just before the nurse came to us, LaCroix grabbed her arm, got close to her ear, and whispered something. The head nurse flanged her arm away, releasing his grip, gave him a dirty look—and walked up to us. So, yes, we have our answer. He wanted to sneak into your room without us. Now, we must find out why. What's his deal in all of this? And who can we trust?"

Chapter 32

Jambalaya Comfort

"It's not a fancy restaurant. But there is plenty of this delicious Jambalaya for the three of us. Maybe with some sustenance, we can rationally figure out what is happening here. Nothing makes sense to me." I say, ladling the Jambalaya into the bowls.

Clark, looking pensive, starts the conversation. "Somebody is going out of their way to get rid of you, Jessica. First, they frame you for the murder of a good friend of yours. They arrest you without due cause, with no concrete evidence, only substantial evidence of your walking stick at the crime scene or at least the disposal site. And when those attempts don't put you away, they attempt to run you off the road, and eventual kidnapping occurs. What is the motivation behind it all?"

"I don't think the kidnapping was planned. That just happened because I survived the ramming off the road. The intention was to kill me and make it look like an accident. Or maybe a suicide driven by remorse. A few more feet ahead or in front of the stumps that held my Jeep, it would have slid into the water, and chances are I wouldn't have been so fortunate. When Little Tim saw me approach the road, he went into plan B."

"And Plan B was to take you to someone who would make the final judgment and execution. Fortunately, you were able to escape." Robert says, his eyes misting a bit.

"Looking in retrospect, I should not have taken the van when I did. I should have waited to see who was running up to us. Once I knew who they were and could identify them, I should have made my escape—that way, we wouldn't sit here trying to guess who the Big Guy or Gal is behind all this." I had to add some lightness. The prospect that somebody doesn't only want me behind bars but wants me dead is too dreary.

"I think Robert will agree that we're glad you didn't stick around to identify anybody, instead chose the opportunity to get away as soon as you could. You're here, and that's all that matters. We will figure out who has an interest in silencing you. That's what it all comes down to. Somebody thinks you know something that could get them in a heap of trouble. That something is most likely what got DuBois killed. Now, we figure out the connection." Clark's legal brain is firing away.

"DuBois and I were good friends, and, in a way, he was my boss. He was not the only person who commissioned me to take pictures, but he was the one whose jobs were most consistent. We have yet to speak in depth about anything or anyone. We would have lunch here and there and discuss an assignment or a promotion he was running, and we would brainstorm about the concept and such. There were no secrets shared or deep personal conversations. For that, I have my gal pals."

"Well, thank you for not considering me part of your close network or circle of trust," Robert adds jokingly.

"Wait a minute, there was one day, maybe a week before he died. We were grabbing a bite at a sandwich shop, and I remember he didn't seem like himself. I asked him what was going on. At first, he said nothing. I prodded a bit more; you know how insistent I can get."

"Yes, I know, but that's a good thing. Continue..."

"Antoine told me he had just been made aware by one of his friends that a law enforcement person was taking kickbacks from a lot of the local businesses in exchange for so-called protection. He was frightened that he may be approached next. A couple of business owners he knew refused to deal with him and currently were in the hospital, under suspicious circumstances."

"Did he name names?" Both Clark and Robert say simultaneously.

"No, he didn't. To me, it sounded like a bad gangster movie. At one point, he turned around as a commotion came from the counter; somebody dropped something. When he turned back to me, he was white as a ghost. He leaned forward and whispered; I didn't know there were cops behind me."

"I didn't notice. I didn't even see the officers come in. They must have come in through the back door. I'm sure they didn't hear you, and you didn't mention anyone, so don't worry. I said to him, trying to calm him down. Right after, the front door opened, and two guys walked in. I turned as they were being loud..."

"Jessica, where did you go just now?"

"I just realized one of the men who walked in was Detective LaCroix. I didn't recognize him at first, as he was wearing a casual polo shirt and jeans, and his hair was tousled, not slicked back as he wears it when he is all suited up. DuBois got up suddenly and said he had to go. He threw some bills on the table and rushed out of the place, running into the detective on his way out. That didn't look suspicious. Now, I remember the piercing look the detective gave me. It was as if he was clicking the shutter and taking a mental picture. How could I have forgotten?"

Robert says. "At the time, it wasn't relevant, but it is relevant now."

Chapter 33

Point of Entry

I'm overwhelmed, and when I feel this way, only one thing centers me. House cleaning, when you have pets, is a must for their health and mine. I'll begin in the kitchen. Oh my, I'll start with the kitchen window. How did it get so smudged up?

"Hey guys, get yourselves a couple of cold ones from the fridge. I'm going to do some house cleaning, clean the house, and clear my head."

Robert is going towards the fridge as I'm starting to spray the windowpane. He halts in his tracks and speaks. "Stop!"

"What? Is there a spider?

"Those smudges, are they on the inside or outside of the glass?"

Leaning closer to the window, I see that the ridges from the greasy smears are on the outside. The window moves slightly as I lean closer to the glass for a better look. Looking down, I notice the window is off the track at the bottom.

"This is how they gained access. They came through the window. Let's call Cecilia and ask her to come over and dust for prints."

Coming in from the outside, Robert observes. "They're pretty smudgy. There may be one or two that look like prints. Of course, they could be yours."

"Oh no, I don't ever put my fingers on the glass. If I do, I make sure I wipe it clean," I answer defensively.

"Of course, if they wore gloves, we're out of luck. But we must do our due diligence."

"Okay, so I'm not cleaning the window in case we can get some answers from the prints. At least now, we know how they got in. I still feel Constantine Carron is involved somehow. He did come in once or twice to bring me samples of his plants to photograph for advertising for his Apothecary. I remember him interested in my walking stick when walking out the back door. He said he'd never seen anything so beautiful. I may have mentioned how my uncle carved it for me, and I never left the house without it when I went walking or hiking in the Bayou on my photography excursions. That's why I always kept it close to the door, never to forget."

"Don't beat yourself up. You can't feel everyone is out to get you. Sharing is part of being human. I have to take this. It's work." Robert says, answering his cell.

I'll call Cecilia and see how soon she can get here. It looks like an intense storm is coming. So far, the canopy over the window has helped preserve the dirt on the window; we may not be so lucky if the wind comes from a different direction and wipes it all off.

Robert is back in the kitchen with open arms. As I walk in for a hug, he says. "I must go to headquarters; some things can't wait. I'll be back as soon as I can. I promise."

Clark is getting up and taking his leave as well. "I better get back; I want to prepare for whatever the detective throws at us. I'm only a phone call and two hours away or less--I have a friend who owns a chopper. I know people." He says with a warm smile and a wink.

As the guys are walking out, my phone is ringing. "Hold up, guys."

"That was the station. The Jeep is ready for pickup. It is drivable. I'm thankful for that."

"Why doesn't that surprise me? There is no way they had any detection or examination done on the vehicle. It arrived only a couple of hours ago. The work order would have yet to reach the forensic department to set up the team to work on it. Somebody ordered the vehicle released. I smell yet another cover-up."

"We can give you a ride. I'll drop Robert off at the airport and then head home to Baton Rouge."

I'm going to call Bobby. He's the mechanic who has worked on the Jeep since I got it. I want him to take a look and make sure it's road worthy. I'm not in a trusting mood. I want to ensure I don't drive off another road and find out the brake lines were cut. He can come and pick me up with his tow truck. If the vehicle is good to go, I'll drive back; if not, he can take it to his shop."

"Great idea. Just relax and be safe." Robert says with one more friendly hug.

***

Okay, here I am, alone with my thoughts in the loving company of TK and TC. Relax? I think not. It is time to plot. Bobby should be here soon to go pick up my cherished Jeep. I do hope it is safe to drive, as I have places to go and people to talk to. I'm not sitting still, waiting for things to happen. I need to figure out why I'm a target for the detective.

I'll start with the sole owner of the Bridal Shop, La Belle Mariée. I've known her for a long time, and she's such an excellent referral for my work. And somebody I would consider a friend, not just a work acquaintance. I hope she will trust me enough to talk to me about any funny business that may be going on. I would feel awful if she were one of his victims. She lives alone and is devoted to her work and her brides. She works late at the shop many nights and is so vulnerable. She's first on the list. I wouldn't want her hurt in any way.

There is Bobby, honking away. Has he ever considered using his cell to let me know he's arriving?

"Give me a minute... Okay, guys, you two behave, and this time, don't let anybody in." I say to TK and TC, knowing they don't care as they walk toward their food bowls and start eating.

***

"Hi Bobby, thanks for picking me up."

"No problem, glad to oblige. So, how did your Jeep end up in the Cops impound?"

"I'll make a long story short. I was run off the road, kidnapped, escaped, got back to the police blockade at the accident scene, and the cops took my car for safekeeping. You would think they would have taken more time to find evidence about the car that hit me. But as it is, it is being released back to me. I know nothing was done. That is okay since I know whose vehicle hit me."

"Why do I get the feeling there is a lot more you're not saying."

"You're right. There is a lot more, but frankly, I'm exhausted. I want to get my Jeep and be back home. But, as mentioned on the phone, I would like you to check it out and make absolutely sure it hasn't been tampered with." I speak.

"At the police lot, how could that be?" Bobby questions.

"Believe me, after what I've gone through since I found Antoine Dubois's body, my life has not been the same. Everything that seemed impossible has been proven otherwise," I say, trying not to involve him more than necessary. At the same time, I let him know why he needs to check my SUV carefully and look for anything outside the norm.

According to the directions, this is the lot I'm to pick up the vehicle.

An officer, looking more like a security guard, waves us in. He is approaching, most officious looking, totting a large clipboard. "Your name?" He barks with a tone; maybe he's been in the hot sun too long. "I need to see ID, registration, and insurance."

Lucky me, I have it all in my bag. You can never be too prepared. "Here you are, sir," I say, handing him the documents.

"Okay, pull over there. I'll pull the vehicle out." He motions. "I believe it is operable. There is no need for the tow truck."

"Can I ask you a question?" I ask before he disappears.

"Yeah, what?"

"Have you been here since this morning or when the Jeep was brought in?

"Yeah, as a matter of fact, I booked it in. It's here on my chart. Why?"

"Was there any inspection done, or did the forensic team look at it at all," I ask, seeing how much information I can get.

"Lady, that's more than one question. Unless you have a badge, I don't need to answer you."

"I'm sorry, sir, I was just curious. I appreciate your time." I say as tactfully as I can.

"Well, come to think of it. Just as soon as I entered the information. A Detective came down and said to get rid of it. I had other things going, so it took me a bit to call you and tell you it was released for pickup."

"You've been most helpful. Thank you." I say, smiling.

He pivots and walks away towards the garage area and waves in the air. How cordial.

"Well, good news and bad news all roll into one. Nobody checked to see what car hit me, showing they didn't care to pursue any leads about who kidnapped me. The obvious answer is they already know who it was. The good side is that nobody was around the vehicle to tamper with it. But, just in case, you're still checking it out for me. That guy doesn't strike me as super observant on a good day." I share with Bobby.

"Don't worry, I'll hook it up and drive it off the lot. We'll go to the Walmart parking lot, and I'll thoroughly inspect it before you get behind the wheel. On one condition."

"Really? After all I've been through, you're giving me conditions."

"I sure am. I'll take a look-see as long as you bring it to us for the bodywork, which it will need," Bobby says.

"You know, I wouldn't take it anywhere else."

I can't help but be sad when I see my Jeep. Here is my baby; the back looks pretty bad, and the side where the stumps kept it from sliding into the marsh will need some work."

"It's not as bad as it looks, easy fix. You were lucky and didn't roll over or end up in the marsh."

"I got stumped," I say jokingly.

"What?" he asks, raising his eyebrows.

"A couple of stumps coming out of the marsh stopped it from going too far down the ravine, and then when I got out of, it slid a bit more, but a couple of other stumps kept it from going in the water."

"Okay, let's take it out of here and check her out."

It's good to know people; Bobbly brought all the equipment necessary to do an excellent job: jacks, blocks to keep it from rolling and up safely, and, of course, a trusty toolbox.

"It looks better than I thought. There is a bend in the chassis, but nothing we can't take care of. Everything looks good mechanically, or mainly something that would make it a hazard to drive—especially the brakes. You can drive it back home and relax now that your trusty Trailhawk is back. Give us a call when you want to bring her in. We can give you a loner while we get her done."

"I'll bring her by tomorrow. I must run around town, and it would be good if I didn't drive the Jeep.

"Do you have some covert, sleuth-type action in mind?" Bobby asks.

"That's on a need-to-know basis, and right now, you don't need to know." I chuckle, but honestly, the fewer people know, the better. It might put them in danger unless they're directly involved in discovering who is framing me and why. And I wouldn't ever do that to good people I treasure.

Chapter 34

Whisper Mode

"Here is your loner. We'll get the Jeep done as soon as possible. Don't you worry. It will look brand new when we get done with her." Bobby assures me.

"A Prius?"

"You said it would be a good thing if you blended in. Not only will people not expect you with this car, but they won't even hear you."

"Very funny," I say as I drive away in whisper mode.

I love La Belle Mariée Bridal Shop. It is charming and welcoming. The staff are helpful, warm, and a blast. Marie, the owner, makes everyone feel at ease. She's dedicated to her brides and will work at the shop till all hours of the night to finish on time or make any last-minute changes the brides request. I don't think she knows the word 'No.' That's why she's so popular and my best referral for bridal photography.

"Jessica, welcome--it's been a while, you've been busy. I hope you are not too busy. I have a couple of contacts for you. You must call them right away. Two beautiful brides will love you to take their wedding pictures, nes pas."

Did I mention Marie is French? Thus, being able to say all that without exhaling and simultaneously making one feel most welcome.

"I've been busy but came to talk with you about another matter."

"But, of course, let's step into my office in the back. It sounds serious, not for everybody's ears." Marie says, ushering me to her exquisitely decorated office with tasteful antiques resembling King Louis XVI's style. Just enough gold to be elegant and refined. It's like stepping back in time and living in a dream.

"Marie, I'm not sure how to say this. It might seem intrusive, and I don't mean to offend, but I must ask."

"Oh, my dear, please say what you have to say. I take no offense. We've been friends for a long time. There is nothing we cannot share." Marie speaks as she steps around her desk and sits in the chair beside me.

"Thank you. As you may have heard, Antoine DuBois was found dead in the Bayou. He was murdered. For whatever reason, I'm a person of interest in the case. Perhaps more than a person of interest, but I don't want to say it aloud."

Reaching out and holding my hand, Marie says. "That is unbeliev-able. Who could accuse you of such a thing? You, too, were friends, good friends. I knew the man for many years. Yes, he was a bit—how do you say-- quirky but had a great heart. I heard he passed, but I did not know any details. I'm so sorry to hear this. How can I help?"

"A detective is in charge of the investigation, determined to put me away for the murder. A few things have taken place. I won't bore you with the details, but I feel he is involved with the murder, the cover-up, and even my kidnapping. I know he is dirty. I need proof."

"Kidnapping?"

"Yes, part of all the crazy stuff going on since Antoine's death. I have my idea of who did it or who ordered it. Now, I need to know the motive—the why?"

"Who is the Detective, who you suspect?"

"Detective Louis LaCroix, do you know him?"

"Yes, I know him and don't think kindly of him. He came around my shop a few times. He was nice and said he wanted to know the shop owners in the area. It was good to have a rapport with people in case they needed assistance. He wanted to know how many employees I had and what hours the shop was open. I told him I often stayed beyond those hours to finish my work. He said thank you, that it was nice having met me, and he went on his way. I thought it was nice of him."

"Well, that seems innocent enough," I said, thinking I may be wrong about the detective.

"Wait, there is more, much more. I worked late for a few nights after the detective's visit. It was after midnight. I was in the workroom, on the sewing machine, it is a trusty one, but very noisy. I thought I heard something, so I went to the front of the store, it was dark. I keep it that way so nobody bothers me. I had my phone flashlight on so I wouldn't trip. I saw a man's silhouette run away from the door through the sheer curtains. The streetlight across the street illuminates the area nicely. When I opened the door, I saw a piece of flat metal lying on the ground. I noticed the door jamb had a chunk of wood missing, and slivers were also on the ground. I thought somebody had tried to break in, but they decided to go away when they saw my flashlight. I called the police."

"Did they send somebody?"

"Yes, they came out right away. They took the piece of metal with them. And they took a report. They told me to close and go home. The door was able to be locked, and I went home."

"And how does that involve the detective?"

"Oh, Mon Cherie, the very next day. The detective showed up. He said he had heard about the failed break-in. He mentioned next time, I may not be so lucky. A woman alone working late in a somewhat secluded part of town was unsafe. But he could help me. He could have extra security in my shop for a fair monthly retainer. To make sure nothing would happen to me or my staff."

"That sounds like a threat to me. Or some coercion."

"That is exactly what my two nephews thought. They happened to be in the hallway and overheard the conversation. They stepped out from behind the curtain. Seeing the detective turned ashen in front of us was precious. You see, my nephews work for the Baton Rouge Police Department. Both are gifted at being about six feet four in height and carrying a muscular frame of over two hundred pounds. Both wore full tactical gear as they did drills with the NOLA department earlier in the day. And had just stopped briefly, and I might say timely visit."

"What did LaCroix do?"

"I introduced them to the detective, told them they were my nephews, and they made it a regular practice to stop by, to check up on me and my business, and visit their colleagues from NOPD."

"You're not kidding about it being a timely visit. What happened next?"

"He shocked their hands and had a painful expression when my nephew, David, may have exerted some pressure on his hand. Stefan held his handshake a bit longer than comfortably, and while looking down at the detective, he said Auntie had all the protection she needed.

And having heard of the attempted break-in, they would inform their friends in the NOPD and the Sheriff's department to make a couple of rounds by the shop nightly to ensure everything was okay, and without any extra cost."

"That put him in his place. He must have been shaking in those super shiny shoes he wears."

"He went from being in control to almost losing control, if you know what I mean. He could not get out of the shop fast enough." Marie said, laughing.

"That confirms some of my suspicions. And as always, it was a blast talking with you. I have a couple of other friends to visit. Au revoir!

Chapter 35

Covert Duo

"Hi, Rene. Can you join me for lunch?" All the revelations with Marie made me hungry—for food and further truths.

"Of course, you want to swing by and pick me up, or should I meet you?"

"I'll come by, meet you by the back door. I'm driving a silver Prius."

"Should I wear a trench coat, a wig, and big dark sunglasses? Rene asks mockingly.

"No need, not this time, but if you have it, keep it just in case. I'll be there in ten minutes." With Rene, no matter how serious the issue, she finds a way to make me laugh.

I'm pulling up to the back door to the mortuary. I can't help but look around. Since I got run off the road, I keep on the lookout for followers, and I don't mean the good kind on Instagram. You can never be too careful. Here she comes. I don't believe she is wearing a hat and dark sunglasses. Her collar is up, and she looks around and crouches as she approaches the car. Leave it up to Rene to go full out to liven up the situation. Her talents are a miss working at a funeral parlor.

"Okay, very funny. I told you there wasn't a need for a disguise."

"What disguise?" She busts out in laughter, unable to keep the 'Spy who came out of the Swamp' façade. "So, where are you kidnapping me and taking me to?"

"No kidnapping jokes, please," I say, giving her a smirk.

"What too soon?" Okay, I'm ready for serious. I know what you're going through is not a laughing matter. But I've always been able to make you laugh and look at the lighter side of the situation. I want all this craziness to be over for you."

"I appreciate it. We're going to Margo's for lunch, a drink, and questions to go."

"So, it's a working lunch since you've taken the new vocation of Bayou Sleuth and are doing your investigations."

"Right now, we're trying to find out who to trust. There is something fishy going on in the department. Good people are working there, but there are also a few rotten apples. I want to separate them and determine which basket they fit in. The only way to do that is to question the people I know. Find out who's been approached with coercive means to pay for security. Who's been threatened by certain individuals, and how much did DuBois know? What knowledge may have got him killed."

"Sounds like a plan. I'll let you do the talking, aka questioning, and I'll order the food and drinks. Okay, partner?"

I sigh at her relentless humor. And know she will always have my back. It's good to have trustworthy friends.

Looking around the building, the Hole in the Wall seems relatively quiet. It's not even noon yet, which is excellent. It will allow us to speak to Margo without the lunch rush commotion. Of course, since this establishment is considered more of a bar with food, most locals don't show up until a bit later in the day.

"This place is dimmer than I remember," Rene states as she bumps into me as we enter.

Removing your sunglasses before entering may help your eyes adjust better. Sometimes, I wonder how much of it is a natural ability to make people feel good and how much is just simple clumsiness. Either way, it's endearing.

I wave at Margo, who's standing behind the bar. She sees us and immediately comes running to us with open arms.

"My dears, how are you? I've heard some of the stuff that's been happening, and I don't believe it. Please come back to a nice booth away from the crowd."

Rene and I look at each other and wonder what crowd she's talking about. Maybe it's the crowd she's anticipating in a few moments. Glad we missed the rush. We are following Margo across the floor to the elevated VIP section above what may be called a dance floor. Wow, this is what I call private and secluded from any crowds, which I'm sure are still to come.

"Please sit. What would you like to have? I'll put in the order, get somebody to cover for me, and then we can talk without interruptions."

Rene picked up a menu as we strolled to the VIP area and is ready to go with her order. "We'll have two orders of fish and chips." And looking at me, she continues. "And two beers on tap."

I nod in agreement, as food is not my priority for this lunch. But as always, I could eat.

"How are you going to approach the conversation with Margo?"

"I have known Margo for a very long time. I was a teenager when I met her. There is no beating around the bush with her. I'll come out and ask if she's had any encounters with the detective and go from there."

"I like that straight, forward, and to the point."

How does she do that? She's carrying a tray with a pitcher of beer, three heavy glass mugs, and a plate of tomato bruschetta. She sits it on the table with ease and grace, as if it were a feather. On top of it, she is smiling away as if it were nothing. That's what I call a true professional in the hospitality industry.

"Okay, girls, this should get you started. Now, let's talk. I can see the smile on your lips and the concern in your eyes. How can I help? You know, New Orleans is a small community. Nothing happens without getting around in minutes. Most of us feel like family. There are those among us who don't belong. They need to be shown the door from time to time. Come on now, you can ask me anything. I'm here for you."

I'm taking a deep breath and holding my emotions back. It's a good feeling to be around people who care. But with all that's been negative around me, it's a bit overwhelming.

"I was wondering if you had any dealings with Detective LaCroix or even if you've met him or know who he is," I ask.

"Detective LaCroix, that 'Son of a Gun.' Yes, I've had the displeasure to speak with him and the restrain not to kick him out of my establishment."

"What happened?" I say, pausing with the bruschetta in midair.

"He strolled in here one evening as we were cleaning up, ready to close the place. He sat at the bar and waved me over as I finished business with my staff. I had an uneasy feeling about him being here so late. So, I told some of my security team to hang on and stay in the back. I assumed some guys would hang back, and the rest would leave out the back door.

I went to the bar and asked what brought him in so near to closing. He said he was driving by on his way home and wanted to see the crowd that left my place at night. He said you can learn a lot when you watch customers stream out at the culmination of the evening. How many are drunk and maybe getting behind the wheel? Is the establishment responsible enough to cut them off, or do they care and, of course, be liable if anything happens? Are any of the customers underage, which would be a violation and get a license revoked? In his observations, he felt there may be some discrepancies, but he was willing to overlook the trivial things if we agreed on a larger scope.

I told him it was late, I was tired, and I was not in the mood for riddles. He said, okay, basically, I can overlook some issues you may or may not have with your patrons and may be able to provide security and protection for a regular service fee. I looked up and saw my security team standing there at the ready in the mirror reflection behind him. They are observant and train intuitives for situations that may pose a problem. I nodded, and they came out. They stood behind him. A couple went behind the bar, and another two stood by the front door. At this point, his face turned from somewhat handsome to hideous. He looked like a caged rat, which is what he is. A couple of the bouncers and security team are former officers. Some are still in the force and work for me part-time for extra cash. The others are retired military personnel. He was dumbfounded when a couple of the officers addressed him by name. This further mortified him, knowing they knew who and what he was. At any moment, his extorsion tactics could be exposed in the department, endangering his career if not terminating it altogether. He didn't know what to say other than force a smile, acknowledge the officers, and scurry out of the place, saying he'd taken enough of our time. And bid us A Dieu!

Chapter 36

The Ticking Clock

Finally, at home, regrouping and recuperating from all the information I had gathered. First, we know that Detective Louis LaCroix is dirty. He extorts businesses to make sure they stay in business without dire consequences. I would like to know if there is someone, I could talk to who didn't pay and suffer repercussions. Would they speak to me? Or would they be afraid to confide and make themselves a more prominent target? There are so many avenues to pursue, and there needs to be more time in my head. The clock is ticking, and eventually, the detective will contrive something with his favorite D.A. and charge me. It's like having a net over my head and waiting for it to fall and trap me, like a hunted creature.

It's good to be home, sitting here with TK and TC. It feels like a suspended reality for a short time--No impending doom, no murder charges, no fear of incarceration. It seems too peaceful to be authentic.

My phone is vibrating across the coffee table, and I'm sitting here laughing as I watch TK and TC ready to attack this alien creature moving on the table. Okay, enough of that. I better pick it up and see who's taking me out of my peaceful space.

"Hello Cecilia, how are you doing?"

"We need to talk."

"Ok, I'm listening."

"Not on the phone. If you're home, I'll be stopping by in a bit. Is that okay?"

"Cecilia, that's more than okay. You can come by any time. I'll have fresh lemonade waiting for you."

"We might need something stronger, but lemonade is a good start." She chuckles, subsiding the seriousness in her voice. "See you soon."

I think she must have the results from Dubois's autopsy. I hope the evidence speaks in my favor to clear me of any wrongdoing and, at the same time, points in the direction of the criminals who took such a valuable life. I can't wait to hear what she has to say.

***

I welcome Cecilia with a hug; after all, she's been so helpful. Hopefully, she'll shine light in the tunnel of darkness where I've been for almost two weeks.

"Please have a seat. Make yourself comfortable. I will get us some nice and cool lemonade as promised."

"I thought you would have something with a little more punch than that." She says, laughing. You're right. Let me share what I've found, and then we can celebrate."

"So, there is a cause for celebration? I was hoping to hear good news. I was so optimistic that I made a pitcher of my version of our town's favorite drink, The Hurricane. Now, let me have the great news." I say as I sit and watch her take a large folder out of her bag.

"I've gone over these results with the utmost care. I triple-checked everything. Undoubtedly, the scene by the bayou where you found DuBois was staged. He was purposely placed where you found him but killed elsewhere.

"Do you know what was the cause of death? Was it my walking stick?"

"The cause of death was partially blunt force trauma, but it wasn't by your stick. There was no evidence that your stick had any contact with the body. Somebody left it there to incriminate you. That was the only purpose. I'm not a lawyer, so why they were trying to place you at the scene is beyond me."

I release a slow breath. Once this all clears and I get my walking stick back from evidence, I won't be harboring a murder weapon in my home. That would be super creepy.

"So, back to what caused his demise."

"Like I said, blunt force trauma caused by a specific hammer type."

"This is hard for me to hear, but I must know all the details. Continue, please." I say while sipping some lemonade and reaching for the tissue box.

"It was an Estwing 14 oz. Forged Steel Hatchet, Drywall Hammer." Cecilia reads straight from her notes.

"That is very specific. How did you arrive at that conclusion," I say, astonished by the precision of the findings.

"I won't bore you with the details, but part of it is by matching the abrasions with different tools. After years of working in forensics, you file photographs, notes, and, unfortunately, memories of different injuries you've come across and the weapons that form them. There were two sites in the cranium that at first seemed to belong to two different weapons. One resembles a hammer strike with rounded edges, and the other resembles a hatchet-type weapon with a sharp cutting edge. There were microscopic particles found on the edge of the sharp incision-type wound. After a close examination, it revealed drywall particles. That's when it dawned on me that it's one tool with two different ends. I took out my comparison chart and got hold of the same type of weapon from our local hardware store. After applying the measurements, it matched perfectly. When they continue the investigation and if they do their due diligence and find the weapon, it should be easy to prove it without any doubt. You see, this was not just any drywall hammer. It had a deformity. At some point, the notch of the back of the hatchet end had worn or broken off. So, there is a unique signature to the tool."

"You know, all along, we thought that maybe Constantine Carron had some involvement in all this. I overheard an argument between DuBois and Carron when I went to the apothecary one day. I also know that Constantine had done some remodeling in his home. Is there a chance the weapon could be matched to the drywall used at Constantine's residence if they find it?" I say with my brain cells on rapid fire.

"Now, you're talking super slough investigation tactics." Something the detectives can dive deep into once the weapon is recovered. That is when the detectives actually want to find the actual murderers. I'm afraid that may not be the case with the detective in charge."

"There is a lot to take in. More than I can wrap my head around. I'm sure Robert will have much more to say about all this."

"That is why I already sent him a file with all this information. He should know and pass the information to the FBI forensic team to confirm my findings. Those were the findings on the surface injuries. There is evidence of a toxin that rendered the victim unable to move. It took a bit to find a match, but it is particularly specific. It is known to emit an odor that most predators detest. Thus, creatures of the swamp do not bother the body. Only one place in town has the combination of exotic ingredients to manufacture this particular poison. The Place is Carron's Apothecary."

"You're brilliant. Thank you. I feel better already." There is more. There is always more. And then it comes to me. "One more question, if I may, did you find out by any chance who broke into my place and took my walking stick."

"Oh yes, I was getting to that. You mentioned Carron, and it was. It was not Constantine but his nephew Jason Carron. He wore gloves for most of it, at least with the smudges when he pried the window off the frame. But after taking the stick, he went out the window to ensure the door remained locked with the deadbolt. When he put the window back in the frame, he got the glove caught in it. When he pulled, he left a trace of fabric stuck in the frame. He must have gotten frustrated and taken his gloves off to adjust the window back in the frame, and sure enough, in the far corner of the glass, there was a viable print. And as we know, he didn't even do that right because you noticed the window was not set properly in the frame, and that's when you called me."

"All this web of deceit and murder around me. And I still don't know why. What was it that DuBois did or knew that made somebody kill him? Why am I implicated and framed for murder? Unbeknown to me, I must be getting close."

"When is Robert coming back?"

"I don't know, soon, I hope. Robert got called on a case, and I won't bug him. Besides, I developed a lead on my own. I've gathered some information concerning our detective. He's been going around town soliciting money for extra protection from local businesses. So far, the individuals I spoke to have turned down his protection advances and had a great backup to ensure he didn't try anything funny. But I wonder if any businesses have rejected his offer and paid the price.

"I have a good friend in the Fire Department. I could talk to her and see if any fires were under suspicion. Usually, arson is a way criminals seek retribution when things don't go their way." Cecilia just provided an excellent lead.

"That will be great. Can your friend be trusted to look into it without alerting anybody until we have conclusive evidence?"

"Patricia works in the Arson Investigations Department. So, those files are at her fingertips. It won't seem out of place for her to look into some open cases or even closed cold ones. What's your next step?" She asks and leans forward in expectation.

"I'm going to call Thomas, DuBois's assistant, and we'll see his cousin Jac, who owns the Airboat rental with the amusement park layout. I wonder if the detective approached him. I have a hunch, and I want to bring this up to people I know who can be trusted to keep it quiet."

"Sounds like a great idea. Just promise you'll be careful."

"It's 'Hurricane' time!"

Chapter 37

One more question

First things first, feed the pets. My number one priority no matter what else is happening in my life. Then I'll call Thomas.

"Here you are, guys, plenty of food and water. It may be a long day. You never know these days what's going to happen.

Priority number two. Calling Thomas, I hope he's able to accompany me today. "Hi Thomas, you picked up quickly."

"As soon as your name popped up, I lounged at the phone. With you, it may be urgent."

"No urgency now, but I appreciate your concern. Would you have the time to accompany me today? I want to speak to your cousin Jac.

"I do have the time; if I didn't, I would make the time. What do you want to talk to Jac about?"

"Are you at the shop or home? I'll grab us breakfast at a drive-through, pick you up, and explain on the way. Does that work for you?"

"It sure does. Secrecy is exciting. I'm at home, and I'll be ready, let's say, in half an hour."

"Ok, half an hour it is. Text me what you want me to pick up for breakfast. Make sure it's car food, can't make a mess, I'm driving a rental. Oh yes, if you look out of your window. It's a silver Prius."

"So, this is like an undercover assignment."

"No, my ride is getting fixed up. Don't let your imagination get the best of you. I need you present."

"Present I am. Yes, Mam, ready for duty." Chuckling as he hangs up.

Another funny friend: how do I attract these people in my life? I'm so glad they're there. At the end of this situation, we will all be laughing.

***

"Thanks for the breakfast burrito." Says Thomas, as he carefully unwraps it, over about ten napkins spread over his lap.

"Don't mention it. I think better on a full stomach.

"I'm ready to be your Watson. How are we handling this interrogation?"

"Thanks for the compliment. If you're Watson, that would make me Sherlock. But at this point, it's much simpler. It will not be an interrogation. I want to speak to your cousin casually and find out if Detective LaCroix approached him asking for money in exchange for protecting his business and livelihood. I've already spoken to a couple of friends who were approached by and denied his assistance."

"So, what do I do or say?"

"You simply tell your cousin I'm a trusted friend who needs information. I'll take it from there. I'm not going to force it out of him. If he has yet to be approached, he'll be on the lookout in case he's approached. He'll probably tell us how he fended off the offer if he has been approached and declined. And, if he has been paying for protection, I will tell him; I'll do my best to make sure that ends."

"It's a Win-Win for all."

"For all but the detective who's treading on quicksand."

"Here we are, let's park here. I didn't get a chance to go for my morning walk. If I don't get my walk in before lunch, I'm sluggish for the rest of the day." Thomas says as he's already getting out of the car and stretching as if he's going to run a marathon."

"This is good. We have a nice tree canopy shading the car. It will stay cool a lot longer. On the way back, I wouldn't mind exploring that path into the forest area. I have my camera, and I could take a few pictures. From the sounds of it, there are a lot of birds in there. Ok, let's go, did you bring your water? Don't want you to get dehydrated before we get there."

"Oh, come on, it's not that far. I can see the water's edge from here," Thomas says, gesturing with his hand as a visor over his eyes. He gets my sarcasm.

There is Jac, walking to the shed he calls his office. Perfect timing. I don't think he has any customers now needing his assistance. Thomas spotted him also and took off running towards him. That guy can move. I'll speed up my walk, but I'm not running. I don't want to have to sit down and catch my breath before I start talking. I'm not out of shape. I don't think it looks proper.

"Here is Jessica," Thomas announces.

"Hi Jac, how are you doing?"

"Fine, Jessica, Thomas said you're here to ask me some questions regarding Detective LaCroix. What is that all about?"

"Thank you, Thomas, for opening the discussion. I thought you were going to be the silent Watson." I say under my breath.

I better dive right in and put Jac at ease. He seems a little fidgety. And now he is crossing his arms. This is an excellent sign that he may not be open to answering questions.

"Jac, I'm going to come right out and ask. Has Detective LaCroix come to you offering protection for your business in exchange for a ransom, I mean a fee?" I wait for an answer, and I wait some more.

Jac is looking around, looking down, doing everything to avoid looking at me.

"Please, Jac, this is serious. You're not the only one he has approached. Please talk to us." I say pleadingly.

"Yes, yes, he did talk to me about two months ago. I had just set up a family to go on an airboat with one of my tour guys. In fact, your friend DuBois was here. The family was a direct referral from him, and he wanted to see them off. He gave them a ride here, and he was going to pick them up after their tour. The detective was very direct; he said it would not be safe for me to refuse his protection or, as he put it, security services. He knew my business was very lucrative. He even knew Terry, my accountant. He has his hands in almost every business in town. He is a scary dude. You would never know it from his daily demeanor, but when he zeros in and looks you in the eyes. You know he means it. I declined politely at first. Then he mentioned my family, my wife, and my two kids. He knew where we lived and where my children went to school. I got frightened when he said my house was in a remote location, and this place was remote enough. Especially when I shut everything down and I'm the only one here after everything closes.

I had no choice but to pay the fee. I've been paying $2,000 every month." Jac says as he wipes the sweat mixed with tears running down his face. "I'm afraid he'll hurt my family if I don't pay."

"I'm so sorry to hear that. It's awful. I can assure you I'll find a way to stop this."

Thomas taps his cousin on the shoulder as I see the moisture in his eyes. "Jac, you can count on Jessica. If she says she's going to do something about it, she will."

"You mentioned Antoine Dubois was here the day you had this disgraceful conversation with the detective. Where was he, and did he hear what was said?"

"Oh yes, DuBois had entered my office after waving the family off. He came in to use the restroom before heading out. When he heard the conversation with the detective by the front door, he stayed in the restroom with the door open. As you can see, it is a small place. A frog can clear it in two hops. Before the detective left, I went to my safe and took out the cash to give to him. I didn't want any trouble. DuBois saw me, and he came out of the restroom. Before I could do anything to stop him, he confronted the detective. DuBois told him he was committing extortion. He was not going to allow that in his town. He knew people. The chief was a good friend of his. He went up to the detective's face, pointed his finger at him, and said he'd be sorry. The detective looked down at DuBois as if he were a bug and spoke. 'You're wrong, my friend. It is you that will be sorry.' Oh my Gosh, I should have said something. LaCroix threatened DuBois in front of me. I was so selfish thinking of myself. I didn't realize he may be responsible for Dubois's death."

My heart is pounding. I had a suspicion. Now that I know for sure, it is beyond frightening. I feel nauseous. I need to contact Robert. Who should I trust in town with this information?

"Jac, don't blame yourself. The thought that a decorated detective would be extorting money from his citizens and be responsible for somebody's death is hard to comprehend. You had to think of your family first. And you had no way of knowing if his threats were no more than manipulation. I'll call Robert. We must get the FBI involved. This is bigger than all of us."

I am dialing Robert's phone; it's going directly to voicemail. This is not a situation where I want to leave a message. I'll keep trying. I must get home. I have the number of his headquarters. They'll be able to reach him and tell him it is urgent.

"Jessica! Today is the day he'll be coming around to collect. What do I do?"

"Pay him, don't do anything different. Act as normally as possible. I know it won't be easy, knowing what you know. You mustn't let on to any changes. Take a deep breath and clear your head. Do this for DuBois." I hug him as we head out.

Chapter 38

Run!

"Look at me. I'm shaking like a leaf. I wish I hadn't told you to park so far away. Let's run." Thomas says as he sprints towards the car.

I'm not running. I need to calm down before I get behind the wheel. I'm taking a deep breath to clear my head and my heart. Ok, why is this car coming in my direction? There is plenty of parking. Oh my Gosh! It's LaCroix. It's time to run, keys in hand. I am beeping the fob and yelling for Thomas to get in the car. The door is not opening. I'm too far. Finally, Thomas is in the car. I can do this. LaCroix puts his car between me and the safety of the Prius. I never thought I would say that sentence.

"Where are you going in such a hurry?"

"I remembered I didn't leave enough water for my dog and cat," I say between breaths and push the emergency button on the key fob, setting the alarm off.

"Stop that. Turn the alarm off. I've had enough of your antics. Get your buddy, and let's go for a walk. We need to talk." He says while driving alongside me.

I would disregard his invitation, except I'm close enough to his window to see him pointing his gun at me. I cannot argue with bullets. I don't want to put Thomas in danger. But, if I force his hand and he shoots me, he'll have to do the same to Thomas, so he doesn't ID him. I'll get Thomas. We have a better chance to get away between the two of us. Let's hope.

"Thomas, get out of the car; we'll walk and talk with the detective."

Did Jac hear the alarm? We can only hope somebody saw something. Right now, we're on our own. The worst, well, not the worst, is that a breakfast burrito may be my last meal.

"Come on, you two, start walking towards the nice bushy area," LaCroix says while putting his gun in his pocket.

"Wait a minute, I'm wearing brand new Hermes sneakers. I can't walk in the mush." Objects Thomas.

"Shut up and keep walking."

"Don't tell Thomas to shut up. What makes you the boss?" I say, trying to deflect the attention from my innocent friend.

"The Ruger in my pocket."

"Oh, that. I almost forgot. Where are you taking us? I'm not walking any further. This is less than a mile from where I found DuBois. It brings back bad memories. If you're going to shoot me, shoot me now. You won't make it back to your car without somebody seeing you fleeing after hearing the shot."

"Nobody is going to hear a thing with all these birds squawking, and my little friend." He says as he pulls the gun out of his right pocket, a silencer out of his left, and starts to attach the two.

"I underestimated you. I thought you were a simple, low-life extortionist. I didn't quite peg you for a calibrating, intellectual murderer. I didn't think you had it in you to do your dirty work. I thought you would hide behind other unsuspecting individuals. You could make deals with, manipulate, and blackmail into doing your dirty deeds." I say, appealing to his narcissistic qualities.

"I've always done my own work. Suppose I'm not hands-on because it's messy. I oversee every detail."

"I'll give you credit for that. A man in control. Impressive. Let me ask you a question. Why me? Why frame me?"

"By now, you'd poked your nose in enough places that you have a clear idea of my side gig. Since you or your friend will not leave these woods alive, I might as well tell you and gain even more admiration from you."

"DuBois always seemed to find himself at the wrong place at the wrong time. He knew too much. I needed to find out where his loyalties lay. His Nemesis was your other friend and contender for your heart. Mr. Constantine Carron. Those two were friends once, but since you returned to town, they fought like cats and dogs for your affection."

"Wait a minute, I never had a romantic interest in either. DuBois was a good, genuine friend, and he referred a lot of photo assignments my way. He knew where we stood and was a gentleman about it. Carron, on the other hand, was an unavoidable evil. He knew many people in town, has a fantastic business, and was generous in paying for the advertising photos I did for his product. When he crossed the line one day. I set him straight: NO means NO. He said he understood and that it would not happen again. All that happened anyway was he sending flowers, bringing a bottle of vintage wine, and paying me a visit at home, saying he couldn't wait to show me some essential oils he had gotten from somewhere in Asia when he sat a little too close for comfort on my couch. I got up and told him it was time for him to leave. That is when he noticed my walking stick and made a big deal about it. Now I remember."

"Yes, I must say, placing your walking stick by the body was his idea. He was a wounded bird after you refused his feeble advances. He thought DuBois had your heart. I'll tell him it was all a misunderstanding on his part. Although, his zeal for getting even with DuBois made it easy to get his dumbfounded nephew and his druggy friend to help in the actual bludgeoning. You know too much sputtering and spluttering, no good for a silk suit."

"Remarkable! All that to cover up your protective services coercion side job. And you enlisted the help of Carron because he felt rejected by me, and that was enough to want to frame me for the murder of DuBois?"

"Carron thought it would be ironic. If he couldn't have you, you would be imprisoned for the rest of your days. A bit of revenge for not giving him a chance."

"He was right. He didn't have a chance," Thomas says unexpectedly. "Neither do you, with them behind you." With the distraction, he runs towards the parking lot in the opposite direction.

LaCroix shoots a round in Thomas's direction. I hear a grunt and a thud. I'm afraid he got him. I'm not wasting any time. Before he lets out another shut, I'm jumping on his back. It should prevent him from shooting, at least shooting accurately.

He bangs my back onto a tree. Oh, that hurts. I reached for his eyes. And with my own eyes, I see a beautiful vision.

Robert leads about a dozen agents in full tactical gear, pointing their weapons at LaCroix. Am I dreaming? Am I dead?

I push back with my legs from the tree and climb down from LaCroix's back. I run towards Robert, embrace him, and behind the troops, there is Thomas. He must have zigged and zagged to avoid getting hit. I can't help myself as I yell take this Bad Blood from my Bayou!

Characters

In order of appearance

Jessica Martin

Robert Hunt

Antoine DuBois

Constantine Carron

Renee Dolton

Clark Roman

Det. Louis LaCroix

Cecilia Rogers

Thomas Dupris

TC, aka Tiny Cat

TK, aka Tiny K9

Also by this Author

Please feel free to go to the link below in your browser and read about
my other books and information for upcoming events.
Enjoy, and thank you for your interest and support.

https://www.juliebelmont.com/books.html

Self Help:

The Path to Personal Success and Freedom

Creativity Business Plan for Artists and Artists at Heart

Live the Life you Love Series, Seizing your Success

Children's books:

Chloe's Journey (Illustrated Children's book)

Novels:

Bad Blood in the Bayou-An LA to LA Cozy Mystery Book 1

'FRAMED'

Next book in the series—Read Chapter 1 at the back of this book

Bad Blood in the Bayou-An LA to LA Cozy Mystery Book 2

'WIDE-ANGLE'

Bad Blood in the Bayou 'Wide-Angle' Book 2

This assignment is one I know I'm going to enjoy, judging from such a picturesque and magnificent backdrop. The wedding that will be spoken of for years will take place here in a month. I am honored for the opportunity to eternalize it with my photography. The opulence of this home is that of a fairy tale. The two-story mansion with a wrap-around balcony on the top floor and a wrap-around veranda on the bottom with elaborate wrought iron is picture-perfect. It looks like a gigantic and enchanting wedding cake from where I stand. The setting is ideal, though it took me about forty minutes to drive across the Lake Pontchartrain Causeway. The twenty-three-mile bridge is one way to get from the primary waterfront in New Orleans straight across north to the prestigious town of Mandeville.

I remember meeting Mr. Eugene Fontaine and his charming and beautiful wife, Olivia, and their handsome son, Ethan, though somewhat shy. The benefit ball they hosted was to raise money for one of their many charities. The family, which has roots in France and Spain, came to New Orleans four generations ago. Their diligent hard work, kindness to employees, and benevolence have made them royalty in the town. Their financial wealth is surpassed only by their joy for life and grateful and nurturing nature to all who meet them. A simple meeting, a shake of a hand, and a gracious promise that maybe one day they would welcome my services have come full circle. I now stand here, ready to walk up to this beautiful residence and become part of the most glorious, happy event: the wedding of their first son, Ethan Fontaine, to the lovely Jane Douth.

One of the double doors opens, and I'm met with a gregarious little lady in her early fifties. She's trying not to be outdone by the little fluffy dog at her feet who has a helicopter prop for a tail. Smiling wide, she apologizes for the little dog and welcomes me simultaneously. Have I passed through a porthole to an alternative super-happy universe?

"Hi, I'm Jessica, the photographer. I have an appointment to meet with Mrs. Olivia Fontaine." I say as I watch Olivia running down the stairs with arms stretched out in a ready-to-hug position. Again, the feeling of an alternative universe.

"Welcome Jessica to our home, and thank you, Anne." She says, acknowledging graciously the lady who let me in. She continues. "Anne, would you be so kind as to prepare some iced tea, or would you prefer lemonade?" She asks, looking in my direction.

"Lemonade sounds great."

"Anne, please bring a pitcher of lemonade to the back patio. Thank you, dear," Olivia says as she moves towards the back of the house. She's wearing a lovely white outfit, a silk-like tank top, matching tied-waisted wide-leg pants, and a floral see-through overcoat flowing behind her like a summer breeze.

She motions with her elegant hand for me to sit in the most inviting and comfortable chair imaginable. Of course, as the city's, if not the nation's most renowned designer, her home depicts decoration perfection. At the same time, there is warmth and comfort about it.

"I must apologize, as my son Ethan and his fiancée Jane will not be joining us for this meeting." She says nervously, which somehow seems so foreign to her initial demeanor.

"Not a problem, we can go over the initial details. In our phone conversation, you mentioned the wedding would take place here. You can show me around, and I can make notes about the best location for the photographs. Would you know how many will be in the wedding party?

"Not sure how that will work out. My son has many friends; although he is naturally shy, he is loved by many. Most of his friends he has known most of his life. Some attended Tulane University with him. By contrast, Jane is an orphan; her parents died in a tragic car accident. I don't know the details; she refuses to talk about it. If anyone asks questions, she reacts emotionally and usually runs out of the room crying. We have no idea how old Jane was when it happened. Or how long ago it took place. As far as Jane goes, it seems it happened yesterday. We tried to find something about it. Maybe knowing what happened would help us understand and be able to help her deal with the loss. It seems like any records of the accident just vanished."

"What you're saying is the typical shot of the groom's men and the bridesmaids' photograph may be unevenly proportioned. I like taking pictures that transcend time and give the bride and groom wonderful, lasting memories. Whatever, that is for the individual couple."

"I'm glad you're a visionary and able to adapt to the situation." She says, reaching out and tapping my hand. Her warmth is as charming as her smile, but her eyes betray her somehow. I hope to be interpreting a bit of stress, not apprehension.

"Jane needs to be surrounded by loving, welcoming family and friends. This joyous event will give her that. It may seem odd, but I would like to take a picture of all who will be gathered-- with them in the middle, front row, and center. That way, she'll know how much love will always surround her."

"That will be lovely, but we have about 100 people attending. Can you get them all in around the happy couple?"

"Not a problem. I have the wide-angle lens to die for."

Acknowledgements

I want to thank my editor, John De Lorez, for his insight and attention to detail. And most of all, his encouragement throughout many years. My family and friends are my most excellent comfort, critique, and courage sources. I'm grateful for the hours they've given me, listening to me reading just once more. I appreciate their patience and support. I must say my nieces, Sara and Luisa, have a lot of patience. This book would not exist without them being part of my team. I must mention my daughter, Krystle, who's my constant inspiration and motivation.

A special thank you goes to the lady who introduced me to Cozy Mysteries at a SCWA (Southern California Writer's Association) meeting. This prolific Cozy Mystery author is Karen S. Walker. She opened the door to a new path in my writing—and I love it. Thank you, Karen.

Last but not least, thanks to my friend Bill Taylor for sharing his vision for the many versions of the cover design. His perspective was most welcomed—most of the time. As an engineer, he has an expert eye for detail and balance.

In Closing

I hope you enjoyed the first book in the series

    Bad Blood in the Bayou-FRAMED.

    I look forward to sharing my storytelling with you.

    To get updates on my work, check the website

    JulieBelmont.com

    And if I may be so forward to ask...please write a review, as it helps guide other readers.

    Happy Reading!

    Julie